Battle of the Guns

The two partners Chet Duncan and Ezra Blain were on their way to Devil's Fork in Colorado, lured by gold – and liquor – when they witnessed the murder of Frank Bennett. The dying man just had time to entrust his daughter Jane into the care of Chet.

Hot on the girl's trail the pair were just in time to rescue her from the clutches of Flint Randall, a wealthy mine owner who had been one of Jane's father's killers. Not content with his own mine Randall was determined to seize the Bennet claim as well.

Now Chet had to live up to his promise and soon he was framed for murder, jailed, beaten up and nearly killed. He was surely going to have his work cut out to save Jane, her mine – and his own life.

Battle of the Guns

THOMAS KELLY

A Black Horse Western

ROBERT HALE · LONDON

© 1950, 2002 Norman A. Lazenby
First hardcover edition 2002
Originally published in paperback as
Fighting Guns by Norman A. Lazenby

ISBN 0 7090 7182 5

Robert Hale Limited
Clerkenwell House
Clerkenwell Green
London EC1R 0HT

Typeset by
Derek Doyle & Associates, Liverpool.
Printed and bound in Great Britain by
Antony Rowe Limited, Wiltshire.

ONE

Chet Duncan rode his bay with the carefree pride of a man born to the saddle. He held the reins high and close to his waist. Skin-tight gloves, now coated with alkali dust, were over his hands. He wore a green shirt and black hat and there was any amount of dust on the clothes. Dark brown pants were tucked into black boots, and everything was dusty. Sweat and dust made a queer mask of his lean face.

Chet Duncan turned and smiled at his side-kick.

'This durned desert jest keeps on an' on!'

Ezra Blain spat dust over the bobbing head of his roan.

'Yep. I got so that I can eat dust. Yessir, mebbe I could make a flap-jack o' dust and rattler's grease! Wal, durn it, I'll be mighty glad to swaller some likker when we hit thet hell town.'

Chet smiled, stared into the heat-hazed distance. 'Another ten miles, I reckon. Devil's Fork is located on the springs around thar. Nuthin' but dust an' gold an' hell-bent *hombres* – so I hear.'

'When we hit thet town, thar'll be two more hell-bents!' cackled Ezra Blain.

Chet Duncan laughed recklessly. He was a complete contrast to his pal. For one thing he was a great deal younger. Ezra Blain would never tell any rannigan his real age – not even Chet. Maybe he did not know his exact age himself. Ezra had been riding the range and the cattle-towns for so long, he was known from Arizona to Montana. He was pint-size, but tough as hell. He had a whisker stubble and only shaved when he found a barber he could trust. And Ezra did not trust many soap-slingers.

Chet was a hard young rannigan. He was a rover and had acted as deputy, top-hand on a ranch, gold prospector and bounty hunter. He was hell-bent, but he barred anything crooked. He had a code and he did not figure to ride the owl-hoot trail.

Smiling ahead at the heat hazes over the arid land, his eyes were blue. Under the sweat and dust, his face was weather-tanned.

'Shore – when we hit Devil's Fork we want to git ourselves a placer an' see iffen there's any gold for us,' he remarked to Ezra.

The old-timer spat again and reached for his water canteen.

'Yuh want my personal opinion consarnin' Colorado?' he barked.

'Yeah. Give!' grinned Chet Duncan.

'Wal, it's a hell-country an' only fitten fer bad men!' snapped Ezra. 'Gold! Heck, I want likker!'

'Guess we'll have to git some gold to pay fer the likker!' grinned Chet.

'Aw, all right! So we start pannin' fer gold when we hit the creek at Devil's Fork!'

That was their intention. That and the urge to wander around the country had sent them over the Devil's Desert from Fort Peter. Ahead there were mountain ranges, now hazy and bluish in the distance. The town of Devil's Fork was not far from the mountain ranges. The creek that curved around Devil's Fork came down from these mountains, bringing the gold dust and small chips that men fought and worked for.

The horses were tired, but they could plod on for many hours at this speed. The riders had water in plenty and the town was not so far ahead, so they were not worried.

In any case, young Chet Duncan was a *hombre* who never worried. He met danger and hardship with that curious serene grin which was famous in a few states. With his grin and the two Colts slung low on lean thighs, he was prepared for anything the danger trail could offer.

For another hour the men rode on under the brassy sun. Then they stopped to dribble water from the canteens into their hands so that the horses could lick the precious liquid. Even Ezra Blain had to admit that water was better than whisky in certain circumstances. While they were standing, holding the water to the animals, a rider tore over the ridge of shale and came into view.

7

Chet Duncan turned curiously, watched as the stranger urged his winded horse to terrible effort. The animal was nearly dropping. The man was feeding steel spurs cruelly.

Then, as Chet and Ezra stared, the crack of Colts lashed through the desert air.

Crack! Crack! Crack!

Chet Duncan's gloved hands moved to his guns and stayed hovering over the holsters.

In another second two riders tore over the ridge after the first man. The two riders pumped more shots at their victim. The slugs were wild, but the men evidently gambled on the chance shot finding a target.

And, all at once, the gamble came off. The rider on the winded horse suddenly pitched off and hit the dust. The two men tore on and flung another rata-plan of shots at the prone figure. Then they saw Chet Duncan as he swung to saddle and rowelled the bay forward. The two gun-slingers wheeled mounts until they were nearly sliding on haunches. Then they rode off furiously in a cloud of dust and disappeared over the ridge. Chet Duncan rode fast to the fallen man. Chet slid from saddle before his bay came to a halt. He ran and then leaned over the man. He saw the blood staining the *hombre*'s shirt and knew the man could not live.

Then Ezra Blain rode up and joined him, bending over the shot stranger.

The man opened his eyes and pain hazed them. He was a white man, dust-covered and whiskered.

'Them – durned – pesky varmints!' choked the man. 'They got me! Tell . . . tell . . .'

His voice faded. Chet held his water canteen to the man's lips.

'Yuh were tryin' to tell me somethin', old-timer?' he asked gently.

Strength ebbed back to enable the man to pant fiercely: 'Shore. Tell Jane Bennett . . . tell her her Paw ain't comin' back! Tell my Jane . . . Flint Randall . . . kilt me . . . him an' his hellion, Myers Stultz.'

'Jane yore daughter?' asked Chet.

'Yeah . . . son . . . find her in Devil's Fork . . . tell her to git Flint Randall an' Myers . . . or they'll git her an' . . . an' trick her outa her gold . . .'

The man's voice breathed into a mere whisper. He coughed and blood frothed on his lips. Chet Duncan liked the sight of blood no more than any other rightminded man, and he was grim.

'Are yuh name o' Bennett?' he asked gently.

'That's me, son,' panted the man, fear of death stamped over his face. 'Frank . . . Bennett. Mebbe . . . I kin ask yuh . . . to tell Jane . . .'

'I'll tell her I found yuh,' said Chet sombrely. The man dragged in air and choked.

'She'll . . . need some help . . . she's jest a gal . . .'

'I'll help her,' said Chet Duncan quickly, before he realized the significance of his words.

The man semed to nod ever so slightly. Then his eyes shut. He choked horribly and in the next minute died. Chet got to his feet and stared over the horizon. Devil's Fork was not yet in sight, mainly because the heat hazes distorted the view.

'Wal, we got to bury this jasper,' said Chet grimly. Ezra Blain shrugged.

'Let's git on wi' it. Them ginks he told about shore must ha' hated him. Who was they? Flint Randall an' Myers Stultz? Ain't never heard o' them. Two killers, I reckon. Wal, we got to ride, so I reckon we oughta git this hombre buried.'

Incredible as it seemed, a buzzard wheeled slowly overhead, high in the brassy sky. No man would ever know how the birds of carrion knew when death was on hand.

'Durn it – yuh hear what I said to this feller?' snapped Chet Duncan.

Ezra stared with piercing eyes.

'Yuh said a lot o' things. What did yuh say?'

'I said I'd help his gal, Jane Bennett,' said Chet slowly.

'Wal, holy smoke, yuh cain't help anyone. We got to pan fer gold. I want likker, remember?'

'I told this man I'd help his daughter,' said Chet grimly.

There was a silence. Ezra watched the young rannigan keenly.

'I practically gave my word,' said Chet quietly. 'An' he was a dyin' man.'

'Shore,' began Ezra. 'But yuh don't know anythin' about this blamed feller or his gal – or Flint Wotsit or the other jigger.'

'All the same, I spoke the words,' said Chet slowly. 'I'll have to do somethin' about it. Iffen a man don't mean what he says, there ain't no sense to anythin'.'

Chet Duncan was perturbed. He had not meant to make any promises, and there was no one who could have blamed him on that score. But he had spoken.

And Chet Duncan was not the man to regard his words as trifling when talking to a man on the brink of death. Chet turned to his horse and threw the reins over, thus ground-hitching the animal.

'We've got to bury this man,' he said. 'An' it ain't no good sayin' it ain't my business, Ezra. I should ha' taken more thought in speakin'. But I said I'd help this man's daughter, so I've got to do somethin' about it. Let's git on with the burial party an' ride for Devil's Fork.'

And Ezra was silent. He knew Chet Duncan; knew him better than any living man.

'Now we aim to help gals instead o' drinkin' an' gittin' gold!' he said hollowly, after an interval of silence. 'Shore serves me right for ridin' wi' a high-falutin' jigger like yuh.'

It was not difficult to bury Frank Bennett. The sand was scooped out and the body laid to rest. The grave was filled in and stones heaped to make a cairn. This would stop the buzzards and coyotes from uncovering the grave.

Some time later, Chet Duncan and Ezra Blain rode on. They were silent. Chet was thoughtful and old Ezra had a resigned expression on his face.

'Wal, mebbe this gal ain't in need o' help!' he muttered more than once.

They hit Devil's Fork some time later, just as the heat of midday was past its crescent. They rode into the ramshackle town, passing the false-fronted saloons and honky-tonks, the stores and liveries. There was a sheriff's office, Chet noticed, and he stopped on an impulse and hitched his tired bay to the tie-rail. He thought he might as well report the death of Frank Bennett and then they could ride on to a hotel and get some grub and a clean-up.

In a passage there was a card which said:

'SHERIFF TOM BRISBANE.'

Chet found the sheriff inside the office. He was a grizzled man of nearly fifty years. He was examining some 'Wanted' posters. He looked up when Chet walked in stiffly, feet clumping on the boards.

'Wal, stranger?'

'The name's Chet Duncan. I'm hyar to tell yuh we rode across a man name o' Frank Bennett who'd got himself shot by two jiggers called Flint Randall and Myers Stultz. This Frank Bennett is plumb dead now, Sheriff. We buried him.'

Sheriff Tom Brisbane opened his mouth and then closed it. He fumbled for the makings of a cigarette. Chet thought he would make one, too. He waited fully a minute until the sheriff spoke. Both men lit up from the same sulphur match.

'Frank Bennett, huh?' muttered the sheriff.

12

'That's who he said he was,' said Chet.

'Kin yuh prove Flint Randall an' Myers Stultz shot him?'

'I saw two jiggers ride up and sling lead,' snapped Chet.

'Shore. Shore, but did you git a good look at 'em?'

'Not exactly. They rode off durned fast when they stuck eyes on me an' Ezra.'

'Would yuh recognize these *hombres* iffen yuh saw 'em again?'

'I tell yuh, I didn't git a good look at 'em. Anyway, the dead jigger ought to know who shot him. He said the hellions were Flint Randall and Myers Stultz. A dying man don't usually lie. Anyways, I'm jest reportin' the facts to yuh, Sheriff.'

Sheriff Tom Brisbane did not look Chet in the eyes. 'Wal, there's plenty o' killings in this town,' he muttered. 'I'll look into it, shore enough. But provin' is is goin' to be mighty difficult. This man Flint Randall owns a big gold vein just outside o' town. He's a mighty clever feller. Anyway, why should be want to kill Frank Bennett?'

'The dead man said something about gold!' snapped Chet.

Sheriff Tom Brisbane laughed, and as he did he looked into Chet's keen blue eyes.

'Goldarn it, Flint Randall's got the biggest bonanza around Devil's Fork filed and deeded! But, thanks fer comin' in with the report. Shore, I'll look into it.'

Chet turned quickly and stamped out of the office. As he went out to Ezra, he thought that Sheriff Tom Brisbane did not seem very enthusiastic about investigating the murder of Frank Bennett. In fact, the sheriff seemed to want to avoid his eyes. The man seemed like he did not relish the idea of tangling with Flint Randall or his gun-hand, Myers Stultz.

And yet there was something inherently decent about Tom Brisbane. He looked a fine sort of man. Yet there was that queer reluctance to take up the inquiry into the death of Frank Bennett.

'Aw, shucks!' muttered Chet.

He joined Ezra outside the office, and they unhitched the horses. He told him the gist of the conversation he had had with Sheriff Tom Brisbane.

'Wal, durn it,' roared Ezra. 'Say, what about us gittin' some likker an' grub! Iffen thet sheriff don't want to look into this killin', what the devil has it to do with us?'

'Nothin' much,' said Chet Duncan grimly, 'except I gave my word to a dyin' man. Wal, we got to eat, like yuh say, Ezra. A man cain't operate on an empty belly, and by hell, my belly is plumb empty!'

'Thet's the talk!' roared Ezra Blain.

They were two hard rannigans, and food and drink interested them plenty.

They found a hotel. It was called Colorado Star, and there was a livery at the back. They placed the horses in the care of the wrangler and then went to the room they had rented.

They took saddle-bags up with them. Chet got busy.

He took out a change of clothing. He put on a clean red shirt – after he had sluiced in the big bowl of water and shaved – and then he got into new brown pants. He brushed and polished his boots until they shone. He dusted his black hat until it looked good again. After a while he was dressed like the prosperous male of the eighties. Ezra watched him with a jeering smile. Ezra contented himself with a wash and a few desultory slaps where too much dust had accumulated on his garb.

'Let's go eat,' said Chet with a broad grin.

'Shore would think yuh figgered to go to a dance or somethin'!' jeered Ezra.

'Not a bad idee – iffen I could find a gal to dance with!' retorted Chet.

'Yuh could find the Bennett gal!' jeered Ezra. A cloud crossed Chet's devil-may-care face.

'Yuh old catamount! Why the devil did yuh mention thet? I got to see thet gal. I ain't got much to tell her, but I said I'd help her. Yuh old idjut, thet gal won't want to dance when she's learns her Paw has bin killed.'

They went out to a Chinese eat-house because the steaks were always good when done Chinese-style. They waded through steaks that made the plates look silly. They had beans with the steak and then finished up with apple-pie and coffee.

'All right,' said Chet quietly, 'We got a job to do.'

'What's thet?' asked Ezra innocently.

'We got to look fer the Jane Bennett gal, yuh old hellion. Let's git goin'.'

They got going. They got the horses out of the livery where they had been rubbed down, watered and fed. As they rode past the saloons, Ezra Blain gulped and moaned vaguely under his whiskers.

Chet grinned.

'Don't let it worry yuh, podner. Yuh kin swaller any amount o' likker tonight. We won't start looking fer a placer until tomorrow.'

They were not exactly broke – although they had been many times before – because Chet carried the money. They had enough money for hotel bills and to buy equipment for the prospecting. Chet had it in his belt.

On the way down the main stem, Chet stopped a prosperous-looking gent in a store suit. He did not know the man from Adam. But he plugged a question.

'Say, kin yuh tell whar to find a gal called Miss Jane Bennett?'

The man in the store suit stared with keen grey eyes. 'As a matter o' fact, I can, sir. It's my business to know most folks around here. But can I ask why yuh want to meet her, stranger?'

'I've got a message for her,' said Chet evenly. He leaned forward on the saddle horn and stared down at the plumpish man in the suit. 'Jest who are yuh, sir?'

'I'm the doctor around here. Doc Wilson. You'll find Miss Bennett most probably at her shack down by the mine. That's way off the trail and around by the cottonwood rocks. Go down the trail, young feller, and turn off when yuh see them cottonwoods in the distance a-growing out o' the rocks. And yuh, old-timer!' Doc Wilson barked at Ezra.

The old-timer sat up in his saddle as if someone had pumped a .48 slug at him.

'Yeah?' gulped Ezra.

'Yuh drink too much an' yuh got bad teeth!' barked Doc Wilson, 'Come an' see me sometime. On Main Street. You'll find my place. I'll fix yuh up.'

And the Doc walked away.

Chet Duncan grinned and reached over and punched Ezra in the ribs.

'Yep. Yuh drink too much! Haw, haw, haw!'

'I ain't had nuthin' but water and sweat fer days!' howled Ezra. 'Hell, he ain't no Doc. I reckon he's a horse-doctor! Bad teeth, huh! Heck, I kin bite bits offen an old Mexican saddle an' chew it tuh shreds!'

Ezra was real mortified. He thought he was good and healthy and harder than rock.

All the way down the trail Ezra kept muttering to himself, and his opinion of Doc Wilson was worse than nil.

They waded the horses across the creek and saw the camps of placer miners. Men were working in the river, making dams and panning the silt. Tents and shacks of the crudest type lined the muddy bank of the river. Right now the water was low. Chet opined that half of the shacks would be swept away if floods came in winter.

The possibility of gold did not concern him at the moment. He found himself thinking of the girl, Jane Bennett. Apparently Frank Bennett had a mine and was not a placer miner. The man's talk about Flint Randall and Myers Schultz getting the girl's gold puzzled Chet. According to Sheriff Brisbane, those two gents had an interest in their own bonanza. If so, why should they want to kill Frank Bennett?

Chet Duncan knew there could be no sensible answers until he talked to Jane Bennett, and even then maybe it might be a bit of a mystery. Well, he would see.

The cottonwood clump was easily located. The big trees stood up in the distance. The horses plodded over the two miles until the curious pile-up of rocks with the cottonwoods growing among them were quite near. They rode around and suddenly saw two shacks. One was about fifty yards away from the other.

Chet rode on slowly, wondering which shack could belong to the girl. Now that her father was dead, the mine would be her own. Maybe the mine was not worth much. Yet Frank Bennett had talked of gold as if the claim was a bonanza. Judging by the shack, it did not look it. Miners often had delusions. Maybe Frank Bennett had been a bit crazy like most of his kind. Yet there was nothing insane about death. The man had died and named his murderers.

Chet was saved further speculation when a girl suddenly appeared at the door of one shack.

All at once, she ran madly from the shack.

A second later a man burst out of the log cabin and tore after the girl. In three, four, five seconds he had caught her. He held her arms.

Some curious sense throbbed in Chet's brain. There was something about the man now grappling with the girl that he recognized. And then he had it. He had seen the broad-shouldered hombre before.

He had seen the man on a horse, but at a distance so that a Stetson obscured the man's face.

This man had ridden down Frank Bennett and shot him. Chet was sure, and yet, of course, not positive enough, insofar that he had not seen the man's face.

Chet Duncan rowelled his horse and rode down to rescue the girl.

TWO

Chet Duncan reached the struggling girl in seconds. He slid from the bay and in three swift strides came close enough to whip out steely arms to heave the man away.

At the touch, the man whipped round. He was a big *hombre* and clean-shaven. Chet got a fast impression of a hawk-like face, and thought there was some Indian blood way back in his ancestry.

The girl – tall, lithe and clad in blue jeans and plaid shirt – sprang away and then stood, rubbing her arms and staring angrily at her attacker.

Chet grinned at the big man.

'Haven't I seen yuh afore?' he mocked.

He saw the gleam in the man's black eyes and knew the other recognized him. Ezra had ridden up, and the man glanced at the old-timer. Chet, watching the jigger, knew that the man guessed they were the two who had witnessed the killing of Frank Bennett.

21

'Yuh ain't seen me nowheres,' snapped the man. 'But I'll teach yuh a lesson, *hombre*. Yuh seem to be a nosey gink!'

He waded into Chet with swinging fists. A right shot out and then a left. They were like hammers swinging. Chet moved with the muscular litheness of a young man. He seemed to dodge the blows with incredible ease. Then his own fists lashed out.

A right slammed on the jaw of the other man. It was like a lead fist ramming a tree bole. The man grunted, but never even staggered. Instead he came in closer, with windmilling fists.

Chet Duncan took two on the chest and received them with a grunt. Chet's fists rammed again at the other's jaw. A right and then a left contacted, and there was terrific steam behind them.

The man backed this time, but contrived to fling a pile-driver into Chet's face. Chet shook it off, drove on with slow, ramming blows, getting through the other's arms.

Both men were well fixed with hoglegs, but they had forgotten them. The big man had figured to beat Chet with fists, and Chet had decided he could beat the other *hombre*.

For some minutes there was nothing but the rasp of breath as both men took and handed out punishment. Ezra Blain looked on keenly. He was ready if the other rannigan went for a gun in a moment of viciousness.

The girl looked on as if fascinated by the trial of

strength. As yet she did not know why Chet had arrived to assist her.

Chet Duncan planted grim blows with some sort of science. The other man hammered more wildly. But the man's punches had terrific power, and Chet realized the great thing was to avoid most of them. And this he did. He was quicker than the other. He got in with a lot of rib-shakers and yet dodged the return blows.

They moved all the time. But the man was going backwards, and Chet was doing the driving. Then, after some more smashing punches at the man's teeth, Chet had the satisfaction of seeing the *hombre* lurch and stagger.

Chet followed up with a fresh burst of strength. The man tried to ward the blows off. Chet planted them savagely. The man was not punching now. He was trying to cover up. Chet rammed away. The man staggered back again. He slipped and Chet helped him down with two rammers – a right and left that contacted with a sound like leather on leather.

The man went down. He rolled for a few seconds and then got up. Chet was waiting for him. He thudded two more gut-shakers. The man hacked at air with one fist. Then he fell again with a rasping cry. He rolled and writhed. He pushed himself up with one hand. He got to his knees. Then with a push he was up again.

Chet let him have it. Two more slamming blows were a finisher. The man fell backwards and hit the dusty ground with a thud like a log falling.

This time he did not offer to get up. He lay and clawed at the ground with one hand.

Even when the man had gotten some breath into tortured lungs, he did not rise. He sat in the dust and glowered at Chet Duncan.

'Hell, I'll git yuh, feller!' he hissed. 'You won't beat Flint Randall an' git away with it! Watch yuh step, hellion! Because I'll be watchin' yuh – iffen yuh figger to stay around hyar!'

Chet stared grimly. So this was Flint Randall! He had bested the man in a fight. And Flint Randall knew that they had seen the shooting of Frank Bennett. But Flint Randall could not know the promise Chet had made to the dying man.

Chet dusted his clothes and walked stiffly to the girl. Ezra Blain watched Flint Randall closely. Ezra did not trust the rannigan. He figgered he was the type to shoot a man in the back. Ezra did not know much about the man, but what he did know he did not like.

'I came riding out to speak to yuh, Miss,' said Chet, with a faint smile. 'I take it yuh're Jane Bennett?'

She nodded. 'That's right. I am. How do you know me?'

'It's a long story,' said Chet slowly. 'This yore father's shack an' mine?'

'Yes.' She was puzzled.

'We've got things to talk about,' said Chet. 'I've got

somethin' to tell yuh – a message from yore father.'
He looked at her keenly. Her brown eyes lit up.

'You've met Dad? Where is he? He's bin gone all day!'

'We'd best go inside yore shack,' said Chet. 'An' I'd like to hear how come this *hombre* was attackin' yuh.'

She nodded again.

'You helped me, so I'll tell you. Flint Randall hates my father, an' I think he knew Dad was away today because he came along to make himself objectionable. He – he – asked me to marry him!'

'Marry thet galoot!' ejaculated Chet. 'Do yuh want to marry him, Miss Jane?'

'Of course not!' said the girl angrily. 'I hate him. He is tryin' to cheat Dad out of his mine. You see that other shack?'

Chet looked along and then nodded. 'Yeah?'

'Well, that shack is part of a claim filed by Flint Randall. It borders on our claim, an' Randall wants to get both. I don't know why, because we haven't found much gold yet on our claim. Dad is busy followin' a vein, but it doesn't pay much yet.'

'Hasn't this galoot got a rich bonanza?' inquired Chet.

'Sure. He has a mine about a mile from here. He has a fine house built an' the claim is a bonanza.'

'So this jigger ain't satisfied with one mine,' said Chet grimly. 'He wants yourn.'

They walked to the shack and she opened the

door. Ezra came with them, leading the horses and keeping a watchful eye on Flint Randall. The man had gotten himself up from the dust and was limping off to one of the cottonwoods where a horse was hitched.

But Flint Randall did not aim to start shooting three people. He rode away, apparently thinking there would be another day and probably more subtle plans.

In the shack, Chet looked around. The mine could not have paid much, for the cabin was a bare, two-roomed affair of logs and mud-filled cracks. But Indian rugs decorated the boards and there was a stone-built fireplace where roaring logs could make a blaze in the winter months. A few desert flowers were arranged in stone, Indian jugs, testifying to the girl's influence. She had been cooking, and on a bench near the stove were two meat pies. Ezra Blain, although he had eaten plenty at the Chinese restaurant, sniffed in appreciation.

'Shore do like the smell o' cookin'!' he ejaculated. Chet Duncan fiddled with his hat. The girl's clear brown eyes were on him. He suddenly realized it was not going to be easy to tell her about her father's death.

But he had to. Naturally she would learn in any case, but he had to tell her how it happened.

'Miss Jane – yuh might think it queer how come I know yuh name but – I bin talkin' to yore Paw.'

'Where is he?' she smiled.

26

Chet fingered the blood on a cut on his jaw.

She moved away and came back with a face-cloth. She sponged the cut with cold water. Still he hesitated. He had lost his smile.

Suddenly he blurted it out.

'Yore father got shot, Miss Jane.'

She suddenly froze, fear leaping through her eyes. 'Shot?'

'He's dead!' gulped Chet. 'We were ridin' fer Devil's Fork when he saw him rowelling his hoss over the desert. 'Nother second an' two jiggers overtook him an' slung some lead. They rode off when they saw us, an' I guess I didn't know what it was all about until it was too late. The jiggers got away.'

She moved mechanically to a chair and sat down as if her legs had lost all strength. She just sat and stared unseeingly. Her face, normally tanned, went terribly white.

Chet Duncan admired her in that moment. Some women might have become hysterical. But seemingly Jane Bennett was a real Western woman. Still she had received a shock for all that.

'Who killed him?' she asked mechanically.

'I talked to yore Paw afore he died,' said Chet, taking a deep breath. 'He said Flint Randall and Myers Stultz had got him. He – he – asked me to warn yuh an' then he asked me to help yuh. I said I would.'

'Randall and Stultz!' she said in a terrible voice.

'Yeah. That's what yore Paw said. I didn't recog-

27

nize the jiggers, but now thet I seen Randall close up I guess it was him who rode off an' left yore Paw. Say, thet galoot has a goldarn nerve to come hyar an' ask yuh to marry him after thet!'

She suddenly covered her face with her hands. Chet looked helplessly at Ezra. The old-timer looked as uncomfortable as Chet. Accustomed to hard living, there was nothing the two men could do or say to ease the blow to Jane Bennett.

After a while she got her nerves under control. This was the way of the west. A woman had to face facts under conditions which would have crazed women in the east. This was pioneer country and women had their own brand of courage.

'Flint Randall wants this mine,' she said fiercely. 'He's simply killed Dad just to get him out o' the way. He figgers he can deal with me easily. That's the reason for his awful talk of marriage! I'd sooner marry a snake! He wants to get the mine for some reason. Maybe he thought marrying me was an easy way out. Maybe he'll try to kill me next or run me out!'

'He won't do thet,' said Chet grimly. 'Because I said I'd help yuh. Yuh kin take me up on thet, Miss Jane. I said those words to yore Paw. I'll help yuh. Must be somethin' mighty interestin' about this claim o' yourn fer Randall to git so dangerous!'

She stared at Chet and Ezra with eyes that still glistened.

'I – I – don't know how to thank you. But I can't

drag yuh into my troubles. Thanks for tellin' me about my father.'

'My name is Chet Duncan,' said the young rannigan. 'An' this old galoot is Ezra Blain. Yuh kin take it we're at yore service. Anyway, I figger I got on the bad side of Flint Randall already.'

'He's a gunman!' cried the girl. 'He has this Myers Stultz as a hired gun!'

Chet grinned and looked down at his Colts. The holsters were shiny with usage.

'Why, Miss Jane, these hoglegs ain't toys!'

'Me an' Chet kin shoot the hairs offen a coyote one by one,' said Ezra modestly.

Chet went back to the main subject.

'I reported the killing to Sheriff Brisbane. But it strikes me thet jigger ain't keen about his job. All I got was a lot o' hummin' and hawin'. Said he'd look into it. Asked iffen I'd really seen this Flint Randall and Myers shoot yore Dad. Thar's somethin' queer about Sheriff Brisbane.'

'He used to be a good man,' said the girl slowly, 'but he's changed lately. I know him – like I know a lot of folks in Devil's Fork. Yes, Sheriff Brisbane's changed.'

'Yore Dad bin away all day?' queried Chet.

'Yes. Oh, Randall must have been hounding him!'

'Guess yore Paw figgered to ride Flint Randall off his trail but them snakeroos caught up with him,' muttered Chet. 'Wal, what d'yuh figger to do now, Miss Jane? Yuh cain't work a mine yoreself.'

29

Suddenly she made up her mind.

'Would you like to look at the vein? Do yuh know much about gold?'

'We figgered to look fer a placer so we could pan some dust,' said Ezra. 'We wanted to make some quick dinero – jest for groceries an' baccy!'

Chet grinned.

'We know plenty about gold. Shore, we'll take a looksee at the mine. Guess I'm interested to know why Flint Randall got his eye on this claim.'

Jane Bennett had further ideas in mind. She could be a determined young woman. On a sudden impulse she said:

'You could work my mine. In fact, we could share the profits. You're right – I couldn't dig gold by myself.'

'Mebbe we might strike lucky!' exclaimed Chet.

Jane had another idea. 'You could become my partners,' she said. 'That's if yuh figure it's worth while.'

'Podners!' exclaimed Ezra. 'Now thet's real nice o' yuh, Missy, but mebbe we'd be stealin' yuh gold. Yuh might strike it lucky.'

'You'd have to work to make a strike,' she said. 'So you'd be workin' for any gold yuh got. Anyway, have a look at the vein.'

Chet nodded, and the three went out into the bright sunlight. They walked over to the mouth of the mine drift. It was a hole in the shale ground. The roof was supported by logs, and the whole working was well-shored up. Frank Bennett had worked methodically.

They walked into the drift, heads well down because it was not more than five feet high. On the way in, Jane Bennett stopped to pick up a lantern. But Chet took it from her and lit the wick with a match. They continued for about twenty yards into the tunnel, and the girl pointed out the thin streak in the rock quartz. This was the gold-bearing ore, but it was not very rich. Then the vein ended up against the end of the drift.

'Dad was sure he'd find the mother lode,' said the girl. 'He said there was every sign. Every day he'd work here and then come to the shack an' tell me he'd soon uncover the mother lode. It was always just a few more yards. But so far there is just this thin streak of quartz.'

'Uh-huh! How about thet claim next to this?' asked Chet, holding the lantern to the roof. 'Flint Randall owns it, yuh say. How much gold does he git out o' thet mine?'

'Very little, I should say,' said the girl promptly. 'In fact, I wonder why he bothers to work it.'

'Does he do any diggin' himself?'

'A bit. But he mostly gets Myers Stultz and another man called Red Barton to do the work. All they have ever brought up is some very poor quality ore. The placer miners do better panning in the river.'

'Yet he hangs on to the claim,' mused Chet. 'Wal, shore seems to be a queer business. Let's git out into the sun. I like the idee of gittin' gold jest like any man, but I cain't say I like holes in the ground.'

'Nope. Shore is too much like boothill fer me!' added Ezra.

They walked out. The girl put her hand on Chet's arm.

'I really meant it – about being partners,' she said earnestly. 'Maybe Dad was right. Maybe there is a lode at the end of the vein. You could work it. I can't hire you or hire any labour. I haven't enough money. But if yuh'd like to take the chance, we could be partners.'

Looking into her pretty face, Chet Duncan suddenly had a mad idea that she would make a marvellous partner in another sense. Such thoughts seldom occurred to him. He had found plenty of zest in living dangerously, and women had seldom crossed his trails.

'Shore, if thet's the way yuh would like it, Miss Jane. We came to Devil's Fork lookin' fer gold.'

'And call me Jane,' she said smiling.

'Mighty fine – Jane. Guess I'm Chet to my friends.'

'Then we're partners?'

'Yep!' Chet looked at Ezra and smiled. 'Thet right, feller?'

'Shore suits me!' drawled the oldster.

'Would you two like some coffee?' asked the girl. There was a silly smile on Ezra's visage. Chet knew the jigger was thinking he'd like some likker in the Devil's Fork saloons. But Ezra spoke up good and fine.

'Yes, Miss Jane. Shore would like some coffee.

Ain't had nuthin' but sweat an' dust fer days.'

They went back into the cabin. Jane became very busy. In a few minutes she placed mugs of steaming hot coffee before the men, and also a hunk of the newly baked pie. Chet Duncan figured he could eat the pie in spite of the steak he had consumed at the Chinese restaurant.

He and Ezra waded in.

A little later they rose, after talking over plans for working the mine.

'Guess we'll git back to town,' said Chet. 'We got a hotel room booked. But take it from me, Jane, I ain't a-goin' to let Flint Randall git away with killings. An' I didn't like the way he handled yuh.'

Ezra coughed.

'Yuh shore paid him off on thet score, podner,' he said.

'Wal, we might git a lead on this Randall *hombre* or some of his sidekicks,' declared Chet. 'So we'll git back to town, Jane. Don't yuh worry none – an' keep thet shotgun loaded!'

And he pointed to the big weapon hanging on the wall. 'Yep; we'll git back to town an' keep a looksee fer this Randall coyote,' said Ezra eagerly.

Actually, he was thinking of the whisky in the saloons! She stood at the shack door as they got the horses and rode off. She waved once and then disappeared inside the shack.

'Figger thet gal is safe out hyar alone?' rumbled Ezra Blain.

'She ain't,' said Chet grimly. 'So maybe we kin order some lumber and knock a lean-to on thet shack. Iffen we aim to work the claim, we cain't live in a hotel.'

'Wal, livin' in a hotel keeps a gent near to the likker,' argued Ezra.

Chet leaned over from his saddle and swiped a blow at the oldster. Ezra dodged it by a hairs' breadth.

'Yuh an' the likker!' roared Chet. 'Yuh kin lay off thet talk or Jane Bennett will figger yuh jest an old saloon swamper! Yuh'll be talkin' about wild wimmen next!'

'Not me!' jeered Ezra. 'I figger whisky is better than them wimmen outa them honky-tonks!'

This was the way with these two. With this sort of banter, they had ridden many dangerous trails together. The terrain was mostly flat sand and shale, but just before they arrived near the creek the ground became rocky. Outcrops and small buttes rose abruptly. Here and there were the strange Joshua trees. In the cracks between the jumbles of rocks silvery cholla cactus grew. To the west of Devil's Fork, the mountains rose gaunt and jagged from the desert floor. They were the home of the slinking mountain lion and eagle. Only a few prospectors, with mule and pack, travelled into the mountains. They were terrible, arid lands, with few water-holes. Only rattlers found homes in the sunbaked rocks.

Passing a lonely clump of rocky outcrop, a sudden rifle shot cracked the silent air.

Chet Duncan's hat whipped away, as if it were attached to a string which had been suddenly pulled. Simultaneously, Chet and Ezra dug steel to the horses' flanks. As the cayuses bounded into a gallop, Chet and Ezra slid from the saddles and clung to the sides of their horses. They were on the Injun side of the animals.

The way they were riding, the drygulcher could see only the galloping horses. Chet had only an arm around his horse's neck. One leg crooked around the animal's flank. The other was in a stirrup. The leadslinger could not see him. True the horses were a target, but that was all. And in a few seconds the horses' hoofs beat a wild tattoo and carried the two men away from the rocky pile-up.

Once around the pile-up and out of the way of possible further bullets, Chet slid back to saddle leather. Ezra followed suit. They reined the horses by a sheltering nook in some rocks. Chet reached for his rifle in the saddle holster.

'Some durn drygulcher tried for us thet time!' he snapped. 'I'll give yuh one guess, podner.'

'Could be a snakeroo name o' Flint Randall,' supplied Ezra.

'Or one o' his cohorts,' added Chet. 'Wal, let's ride back. Mebbe we kin sling some lead with thet *hombre*.'

'Shore looks like we got on the wrong side o' thet

rannigan,' growled Ezra. 'Hell, when do we git to thet likker? Fust it's one thing, an' then it's 'nother!'

With a slight, reckless grin, Chet Duncan rode his horse out of the nook. He took the lead. He rode forward at a walking pace, keen blue eyes glinting as he stared all around.

Slowly, they rode around the rocky pile-up. They were still chancing a bullet from the drygulcher. The man would be hidden. He could snap off a shot and have the element of surprise.

It was silent again. There was hardly any movement in the air. Heat was bringing sweat to the horses again. Only a mile away lay the creek with its hundreds of placer miners encamped along the banks. Yet somewhere in the rocky pile-up lay a cunning man, ready to kill without compunction.

The horses jigged on. They were under control, having got over the fright caused by the sudden shot. Chet swept the ridges of rock with eyes that noticed every little detail.

The next shot rang out with the same abruptness, but not without warning to Chet Duncan.

A split second before the bullet cracked through the air, he saw the movement of the man. High on a ledge among the boulders he had seen the man's head move as he rose slightly to get a better view of his targets.

Chet whipped his rifle up and fired with incredible speed even as the drygulcher's shot rang out!

The two shots cracked the air. But the attacker had

been too hasty. His bullet hissed over Chet's head. Then Chet and Ezra were pumping shots at the rocky ledge. The man had evidently dropped flat out of sight.

Chet rode away from Ezra with the idea of circling the drygulcher. As Ezra pumped some shots up to the rocks, Chet reloaded. They had the drop on the man now. He dare not raise himself while the rataplan was throwing steel-jacketed shells all around him.

Chet Duncan rode around the pile-up and suddenly saw the man scrambling down the boulders. He was making for a horse evidently hitched in some sheltered spot.

Chet triggered two shots, but the man jumped like a mountain goat for cover. Chet did not see him again, and he could not see the *hombre's* horse.

The next glimpse of the man was when the fellow ran like mad for an overhanging bluff. Chet guessed the horse was hidden there. The man afforded only a second's glimpse. Chet spurred his horse forward to round the scattered pile-up of boulders and wind-worn rocks.

All at once the man rode out of the rocks. He was feeding steel to the mount pretty cruelly. He was trying to make his getaway.

Chet urged his bay after the man. Chet figured Ezra was just behind him.

The young rannigan suddenly knew he had the drygulcher in a bad jam. Chet rose in the stirrups and aimed. The bay steadied as if knowing what its master wanted.

37

Chet Duncan triggered. The man ahead jerked in his saddle as the rifle cracked. Then, slowly, he fell side ways. His foot caught in the stirrup and the horse dragged him some yards. Then the boot freed and the man slithered to a halt in the dust.

'Got him!' exclaimed Chet grimly.

In another second he rode up and halted his bay. He stared down grimly at the prone man. The *hombre* did not move.

Ezra rode up and brought his horse to a slithering halt. He peered at the body.

'Is thet jigger Flint Randall?'

Chet got down. He turned the man over, stared.

'Nope. It ain't Randall. Too bad.'

'Is the galoot dead?' asked Ezra hopefully.

Chet looked at the patch of blood between the man's shoulder blades.

'If he ain't dead, he kin count the seconds left to him,' he said grimly. 'Wal, he figgered to kill us, so it's on his own head.'

He examined the man further and knew that the drygulcher was dead. He had ceased to breathe. His heart was not pumping any longer.

The man was a lantern-faced border ruffian in dirty range clothes. He wore two Colts. Chet took one out of the holster, on a sudden impulsive idea, and stuffed it inside his shirt.

'We're goin' to have another burial party,' he told Ezra.

'Hell, I'm shore tired o' diggin' graves!' bawled

the old-timer.

'We can't leave a man to the buzzards.'

'I reckon this jigger would shore ha' left one o' us to the buzzards!' snapped Ezra.

'Mebbe. Git down of thet hoss an' lend me a hand. It won't take long to make a grave. A grave fer a coyotte, I guess!'

'He musta bin one o' Flint Randall's jiggers,' declared Ezra. 'Ain't no one else in these parts who wants us out o' the way.'

'He's a gunny,' admitted Chet. 'Randall must have got on to him mighty quick an' told him to lie in wait for us. Randall must ha' guessed we'd ride back this way.'

'Thet galoot shore got it in bad fer us,' grumbled Ezra.

They got to work on the grave for a coyote. Soon the man was laid to rest. He had lived by the gun and died that way. In burying him, Chet and Ezra were doing the right thing. It was the last thing that would ever be done for the drygulcher.

Finally, Chet climbed back to his saddle. He stared over the arid land, not seeing the heat hazes that shimmered everywhere.

'We'll find Randall,' he muttered. 'I got to hand him this galoot's gun.'

THREE

Chet Duncan and Ezra Blain rode into Devil's Fork and went along to the hotel. They put the horses in the livery at the back and got two fresh animals. There was no point in tiring the other two cayuses. Then the two hard rannigans rode out of town again.

They had received directions on how to find Flint Randall's bonanza from the liveryman.

Some time later, riding the fresh horses, they came close to the mine. The drift was located in a bluff known as red barranca. The shaft went into the red hill, and a small gauge line fed the drift. Wagons stood on the line and some were filled with ore. There were shacks nearby to house ore-crushing plant. There was a clapboard office building, and then, behind that, lay Flint Randall's home. The house was clapboard painted white and looked large and prosperous. Nearby was a corral for Randall's remuda. A few horses were feeding.

'Shore got himself a nice place,' remarked Ezra.

41

'Yeah. An' he cain't let alone a gal an' her Paw,' snapped Chet. 'Thet's the way lust for gold gits some *hombres*. They cain't git enough money. I guess money means power to them. Though I don't understand how come Randall wants Jane's mine so much.'

'Must be gold thar,' said Ezra slowly. 'Cain't be anythin' else.'

'Yeah, I guess that must be it.'

But, of course, that was just speculation. Frank Bennett had not got much gold out of the mine, and he was an experienced miner. Still the man had talked about gold with his dying breath. Well, time would tell.

Chet rode deliberately to the white clapboard house. He rode tall in the saddle. He reached a tie-rail and dismounted. Ezra followed suit. They hitched the animals to the rail, and then went up the porch steps. They had hardly reached the porch when the door opened and Flint Randall walked out stiffly.

'Yuh two agen! What the hell d'yuh figger yuh're doin' hyar?'

'Ain't yuh surprised to see us, feller?' drawled Chet.

Flint Randall's lips were drawn back to reveal strong, yellow teeth.

'Why the devil should I be surprised?'

Chet slowly brought out the gun from his shirt. He turned it over, looked at it and then threw it at Flint Randall's feet.

'Thet's yore drygulcher's gun. He won't need it any more. He's buried now. Who was he, *hombre?* Was he Myers Stultz?'

Flint Randall lowered his black eyes to stare at the Colt on the porch floor. Then a slow grin went over his hawk-like face. He uttered a sneering laugh.

'I don't know what the blazes yuh're talkin' about. Ef yuh figger to see Myers Stultz, I kin get him for yuh.' Flint Randall paused and then shouted: 'Myers! Two gents want to see if yuh're alive!'

Another pause and then a medium-sized man walked through the door. He halted, stared at Chet and Ezra.

He had no smile or much expression. He was a blond man, with a stubble of blond beard. Light blue eyes stared at Chet and Ezra.

'Yeah?' said Myers Stultz.

'These hellions thought yuh was dead,' jeered Flint Randall.

Myers Stultz did not smile. His hands hovered near his gun butts.

'This the two yuh told me about, boss?' he asked gratingly.

Flint Randall scowled.

'Yeah. They got ideas, Myers. I don't have to say anythin' more. Yuh know what I mean.'

Chet drew a deep breath. His grin was still in evidence. He had faced tougher, rougher, *hombres* than these with the same smile.

'All right, Randall. So Myers ain't dead. But that

jigger yuh sent to blast us ain't so healthy. Maybe he was jest a hired gun. It don't matter to me. An' let's git some matters straight, Randall. Yuh got yore loop tangled around Jane Bennett. Yuh killed her Paw. Yuh may be gittin' away with thet fer the moment, but it won't last. I don't want to see yuh near Jane Bennett. Me and Ezra Blain hyar have gone into podnership with Jane an' we figger to work her mine. She's told us plenty about yuh, Randall. My name's Chet Duncan. Got all thet?'

Flint Randall's eyes suddenly gleamed.

Chet knew the man's mind. With the speed of light he scooped his Colts out. His hands were just a blur. Flint Randall stopped moving. His hands had got to his gun butts and no further. Behind him, slightly to the side, Myers Stultz was in the same position.

'Don't draw yore hardware!' snapped Chet. 'I'd have to squeeze these triggers. Thet would kinda hurt yuh guts!'

Randall was plainly amazed at the speed of the draw. Slowly his hands moved away from his holsters. 'There's law in these parts,' he grated. 'I'll have Sheriff Brisbane see yuh two out o' this town. I kin see yuh're jest a pair o' gunslingers. Devil's Fork don't want yuh kind.'

'My, my, how yuh talk!' mocked Chet. 'Anybody would figger yuh was the sheriff. An' yuh seem to figger Sheriff Brisbane will take notice o' yore fool talk.'

Black eyes glittered again at Chet.

'Git offen this property an' take a tip. Git out o'

this territory. If yuh don't, yuh won't live long.'

'Like Frank Bennett!' said Chet harshly. 'Listen, h*ombre*, I don't scare! Yuh're jest a mangey coyote. Yuh're a murderer. Yuh jest hounded down Frank Bennett. Yuh didn't kill him in a fair gun-fight. Yuh after his daughter's mine. Wal, yuh got us to reckon wi'. Shore we're gittin off this property. Kinda smells like a lot o' polecats was around!'

'Hell, yuh wouldn't talk like thet iffen yuh didn't have a gun on us!' grated Flint Randall.

Chet promptly stuck his Colts back in the holsters. 'I'm still talkin', Randall. I figger yuh're a no-good snakeroo!'

But Flint Randall made no move to his guns. Only his black, Indian eyes glittered. Behind him, Myers Stultz froze in the same manner.

'All right. Let's go,' said Chet, and with the words the guns were in his hands again. It was a miracle of gun-scooping. His hands just moved in a blur.

With Ezra Blain, he backed to the horses. He did not trust the two men on the porch. They were obviously yellow-streaked, but that would not prevent them from shooting a man in the back.

But getting out did not present much problem to Chet and his sidekick. They got to saddle leather and rode out with guns still prominent. Only when they were out of range did the two men stick hardware back to holsters.

'Wal, now thet jigger will shore hate us like pisen,' remarked Ezra.

45

'Let him.' Chet grinned recklessly. 'We've prod-ded worse snakeroos than thet afore.'

'Shore. Wal, what about thet likker? I think I mentioned it afore.'

'Mentioned it!' roared Chet. 'Yuh old hellion, all yuh done since we hit this town is moan about yuh draped likker! Goldam it, we'll go git some jest to shut yuh rat-trap!'

'An old galoot like me needs good likker,' complained Ezra.

They rode into Devil's Fork and entered a saloon. Chet had a whisky with Ezra, but he was thoughtful. He didn't like the position. Even as he drank, he was thinking of Jane Bennett back on the claim, sitting all alone in her cabin. He realized the situation was not good.

Ezra made noises of great relish as he drained his glass. He smacked his lips and ordered another – and one for Chet. The saloon was full of assorted charac-ters – miners paying for their drinks with gold dust, a few cowboys from the distant spreads to the east, where the grass grew fair enough to support some steers. Some were drinking and a few were gambling on a corner table with the inevitable black-coated professional cardsharp.

'Shore is mighty good to a dusty-throated *hombre*!' boasted Ezra.

He drained his glass again and was about to beckon to the bartender when Chet gripped his arm.

'Let's git goin'.'

'Heck, I ain't started yet!' protested Ezra.

'Yuh've had enough to fill yore craw fer the time bein',' said Chet. 'I'm not happy about Jane. That no-good catamount might start somethin' against thet gel. We got to be thar.'

'Holy rattlers! I ain't had enough likker to fill my holler tooth!' complained the oldster.

'Git a bottle,' suggested Chet.

That idea brightened Ezra Blain, and he beckoned to the barkeep.

A minute later they went out of the saloon, with Ezra hugging a bottle of raw rye whisky. They rode to the hotel, and Chet went in to get the saddle-bags. Ezra got the bay and the roan and changed saddles over. A few minutes later they rode down the trail in the direction of Jane Bennett's mine. Ezra was hugging the bottle which he had inside his dusty old shirt, and he was singing an ancient Mexican song. He did not know half of the words or the lingo, but that did not worry him much.

Chet Duncan must have had a hunch, for when they rode near to the Bennett mine two hell-bent *hombres* were sitting on horses and pot-shotting at the shack with Winchesters.

The two men were no less than Flint Randall and Myers Stultz. Then Chet heard the roar of a shot-gun come from the cabin window and knew that Jane was keeping the hellions at a distance. But the shot-gun had only a limited range and the shot fell far short of the two men with the rifles.

47

Chet and Ezra tore in with barking rifles. Seeing them, Flint Randall and his sidekick immediately rowelled their mounts and raced off. As they did, another man ran for a horse, coming from behind the shack. He had obviously been working round to enter the shack while Flint Randall and Myers Stultz covered with rifle fire and attracted Jane's attention.

Chet sped the man on the way with a rataplan of rifle fire. Then, with Ezra, he rode up behind the shack and jumped down. Before going inside, he stared over the arid land, but Randall and his cohorts had apparently ridden off. The hellion wanted to make trouble, but apparently he did not intend to risk his skin too much.

Inside the shack, he found a distraught girl. He took the shot-gun from her and laid it to one side. He held her arms.

'They're tryin' to scare me away!' cried the girl. 'All that shootin' is just to scare me. Randall wants this claim!'

'He ain't a-goin' to git it,' declared Chet. 'Maybe he was tryin' to raise a scare. I guess thet's why he rode off. He don't figger to play lead-swinging fer keeps. But we don't scare easy, do we, Jane?'

Brown eyes smiled at him. He was grinning serenely, and it was infectious.

'We don't scare,' she repeated.

He told her all that had happened since they had left her. He told her about the drygulcher who had met his just fate, and he described how they had gone on to Flint Randall's home.

'Thet jigger has a real bonanza,' he said, 'and yet he ain't satisfied. Guess it's jest plain greed. Wal, tomorrow we start work on yore mine. We'll follow thet vein a bit further.'

'It might just peter out,' cried the girl. 'That happens, doesn't it, after weeks of work?'

'Guess we'll see,' said Chet gravely.

Ezra uncorked his bottle. 'What about a drink to us podners?' he suggested.

'Yuh kin have a drink an' then saddle yoreself to yore roan,' said Chet, grinning. 'Somebody has to ride into town an' order some lumber. We got to make for a bit extry room on this shack iffen we want to live hyar an' work.'

And that was the way it had to be. Ezra Blain groused plenty, but he rode off later for Devil's Fork. When Ezra returned later he had apparently sampled some more of the saloon's drink, for he was plumb hilarious. But Ezra Blain was never the worse for his drink. He could ride and shoot even after a prolonged binge.

The lumber would arrive the next day. It was ordered and would have to be paid for when it arrived. In the meantime, Chet went inside the drift to further examine the vein. He left Ezra with the girl.

By the light of a lantern, Chet Duncan examined the thin streak of gold-bearing, ore. Right up against the face of the drift, the vein continued into the shale and rock. Chet stared, wondering what lay ahead in the dark mass of rock and shale. Was there a mother lode? Had Flint Randall some inkling of this? If so, how had he got his knowledge?

There were various points he could find no answer to. But he was determined to mine the claim. He figured to follow the vein until it vanished, went into Flint Randall's adjoining claim, or materialized into a bonanza.

Chet and Ezra spent that night on the floor of the shack living-room with two blankets apiece.

The next day the lumber arrived on mule wagons, sent out by the merchant in Devil's Fork. It was unloaded and Chet paid for the supplies. Half an hour later the wagon had departed, the two men began work on the addition to the shack. All they wanted was another room, and tastes were simple in the pioneer west. Half-way through the morning's work, Chet Duncan was surprised to see Sheriff Tom Brisbane ride up to the mine. The sheriff sat his horse, leaning heavily on the saddle horn, and surveyed the work with his grey eyes.

'I bin makin' inquiries,' said the sheriff. 'Flint Randall an' Myers Stultz were nowhere near the desert yuh mention when Frank Bennett was kilt. They were in town. They've got friends to prove alibis.'

'Is that what Randall told yuh?' snapped Chet.

'I've bin makin' the inquiries myself!' rapped Sheriff Brisbane.

'Seems Flint Randall got a lot o' good pals,' retorted Chet. 'Includin' the sheriff o' this territory.'

50

'Thet ain't called for,' said the other heavily.

'No? Wal, forget it, Sheriff. I kin handle Flint myself – with Ezra's help, shore.'

'This jigger yore side-kick?' asked Sheriff Brisbane.

'Yep. Meet Ezra Blain. Jest pint-sized, but he knows his onions.'

The sheriff nodded.

'I bin hearin' yuh done some shootin' yoreself,' he continued. 'Yuh buried a jasper name o' Del Parker.'

'Shore we buried him,' said Chet easily. 'He was plumb dead.'

'Yuh shot him, huh?'

'Yep. He figgered to drygulch us, but he got in the way of our return lead. Is thet agin the law, Sheriff? Is it agin the law in these parts to shoot in self-defence?'

'Flint Randall said yuh jest gunned the man down,' mumbled Sheriff Tom Brisbane.

'Wal, yuh listenin' to a durned snake talkin', Sheriff. An' there ain't nothin' yuh kin do about thet drygulcher. He's dead, an' we ain't.'

And it seemed that Sheriff Brisbane did not want to pursue the matter further. Instead his grey eyes turned to Jane as she came out on hearing the voices.

'Howdy, Miss Jane. I – I – guess I'm sorry, mighty sorry, about yore Paw. Guess there ain't nothin' I kin do until – until – I find out who kilt him . . .' and the sheriff's voice trailed off.

'Flint Randall and Myers Stultz killed him!' she cried.

'I cain't prove thet,' mumbled Tom Brisbane.

'Yuh mean yuh don't want to try!' returned the girl.

The sheriff took a deep breath. 'Why don't yuh sell this claim, Miss Bennett? Mebbe yuh'd be happier if yuh sold an' went away. This territory ain't no good for a gal on her own.'

'Who'd I sell to?' exclaimed Jane.

'Mebbe Flint Randall would be interested,' muttered the sheriff. 'He's got a claim nearby, though it don't pay any. Yeah, mebbe he'd take this claim offen yore hands.'

'I think you've been sent by Flint Randall to persuade me!' cried the girl.

'I ain't speakin' fer Randall!' snapped Sheriff Brisbane. 'I'm tryin' to help yuh.'

'Wal, Jane has got us to help her,' said Chet quietly. 'Yep. Shore got us,' added Ezra. 'We figger to work this mine as podners.'

'All right. Have it yore own way!' rasped the sheriff, and he wheeled his horse and fed steel rowels. In a minute he was just a dark shape on the yellow, arid land.

'I reckon Devil's Fork ain't gittin' value fer money in their sheriff,' said Chet angrily. 'Thet galoot is with Flint Randall!'

Whether the accusation was right or wrong, there was little Chet Duncan could do about it. They got on with the work of building the extension.

Later, when the sweltering heat of midday had passed, Chet rode into town in order to buy some special prospecting equipment. He wanted a new drill. The old one was broken and not much use. With a new drill he could take samples of the vein which reached into the virgin rock.

On the way. he passed the sheriff's office and he happened to glance at the porch.

Flint Randall was standing beside Sheriff Tom Brisbane, and they were in the act of tacking a 'Wanted' poster to the board.

High in the saddle, Chet could see the bold wording of the bill. He sensed it had been newly-printed for the ink was hardly dry. Then his eyes caught the large lettering, and every muscle went taut in his body.

He got a swift impression of the words: WANTED. FOR ROBBERY AND MURDER. CHET DUNCAN AND EZRA BLAIN, wanted by the SHERIFF OF CREEKTOWN, ARIZONA, from this day, 19th June, 1889 . . .

Then the print ran smaller.

But Chet had seen enough. It leaped through his mind that this was the most blatant frame ever possible. The poster had just been printed. And the facts were brazenly incorrect and libellous.

'Thar he goes!' shouted Flint Randall, and then followed a jeering laugh.

Chet Duncan whipped his Colts and blazed a number of slugs into the poster. The roar of blazing guns shattered the air. The next moment the young, enraged rannigan rowelled his bay and galloped down the main stem. Dust billowed under pounding hoofs. He threw the horse around a bend and rode hell-for-leather out of Devil's Fork.

He knew the frame-up was simply and solely to give any *hombre* an excuse for throwing lead his way. No doubt the poster mentioned a reward. This was Flint Randall's work, but it could not have been possible without Sheriff Brisbane's aid. Tacked outside the sheriff's office, the poster looked authentic.

Chet got the plan. Randall wanted him and Ezra out of the way – dead. He had made them wanted men – wanted for crimes they certainly had not committed. And, if captured, here would be no chance of a trial. In fact, if Randall had his way, they would not even be taken as prisoners. They would be conveniently shot, and explanations, if any, could follow later.

Devil's Fork was lawless, sure enough. And Tom Brisbane was in Flint Randall's pay. This exploit proved it.

The bay's hoofs beat a tattoo that took Chet out over the arid lands at a fast lick. He flung a glance backwards and thought he detected signs of pursuit. He had got a good lead. He thought he saw the tell-tale cloud of dust way back behind him. Maybe it was Randall and some others. The poster would trick any citizen of Devil's Fork into chase. In fact, there was nothing to stop a posse from being formed for the purpose of getting Chet Duncan and Ezra Blain.

Chet cursed the lawlessness of the place. He was now a wanted man – along with Ezra. Unless he could expose the frame-up, he would not dare go into town. There was only one way to get free of such a false charge, and that was by contacting the sheriff of Creek town, Arizona, and getting the truth. But that would take time.

Chet rode the bay fast to the Bennett mine and then leaped to the ground. He rushed up to Ezra Blain.

He began to shout explanations for his sudden appearance.

'Say, Ezra, we're framed! I've jest seen a poster on the sheriff's office an' it says we're wanted for robbery an' murder in Creektown, Arizona!'

'I ain't never bin in Creektown, Arizony!' bawled the startled Ezra.

'Thet may be plumb right,' said Chet grimly. 'Where's Jane?'

'She took a buckboard out to visit some nesters fer to git some fresh vegetables!'

'We got to ride,' said Chet grimly. 'We've got some jiggers on our trail right now. Hit leather, podner!'

FOUR

There was no doubt about it, they had a posse on their trail. As Chet and Ezra rode out on a trail across the arid lands, the cloud of dust followed them. It seemed there were several riders, and not just Flint Randall and the sheriff. Who the riders were, as individuals, Chet and Ezra could not know.

It was useless to stop and argue. A slug might silence their share of the arguing. And Chet did not feel inclined to throw lead at men other than Flint Randall's rannigans.

The task was to shake off the posse and then make plans.

Chet Duncan sat low in the saddle and rowelled the bay. Ezra rode stirrup to stirrup. They flew across the sand and shale terrain, making for the beginning of the foothills. The chase would be furious for a few miles. They hoped to lose the pursuers once the foothills were gained.

But it was not to be.

All at once Ezra's roan stumbled and fell. The animal had put a hoof in a hole. It was a wonder the horse did not break a leg. But Ezra was unseated as the animal crashed terribly to the shale.

Chet reined his bay immediately. He turned the horse and rode back. Ezra was sitting up in a daze, while the terrified horse got to its legs and reared. For a moment Chet thought the animal might stamp its hoofs down on the old-timer. But Chet calmed the horse. Then he got down and helped Ezra to his feet.

'Goldarn it!' muttered the oldster. 'I shore feel groggy!'

He swayed and Chet had to support him. Then Chet stared at the cloud of dust. Before it were a number of riders, coming on with remorseless speed.

'Kin yuh make it?' panted Chet.

He tried to hoist Ezra to the roan, but the animal shied away. Then Chet tried to get the old-timer on to his own bay. He got to the saddle and leaped up behind him. Chet fed spur steel to the cayuse. As the bay started forward gamely under the double load, the roan trotted along, too.

But the possemen were terribly near. The double load slowed the bay considerably. As Chet flung a backward glance, he saw the possemen had spread out to overtake them on all sides.

The chase could have only one end. The foothills were not reached before guns began to bark and slugs whine through the air. Chet could not stop now to try the roan again with Ezra in the saddle. And a few riders were almost abreast of them on both sides. Any moment Chet expected a slug to take him in the back. It was a grim feeling.

But the tearing slug did not come his way, although some *hombre* was pumping a few wild shots in his direction.

Then in swift seconds the outriders closed in. Grimly, Chet Duncan realized there was nothing for it but to rein in and face the men. The bay was blowing badly, and he did not want to wind the gallant horse.

He reined and came to a halt. Almost all at once, he was surrounded and guns pointed from all directions. One Colt exploded, and the bay reared as the slug tore past.

'All right!' grated Sheriff Tom Brisbane's voice. 'Yuh kin stop shootin' men. We've got these galoots.'

Chet turned his head, saw Flint Randall grinning jeeringly. With him, almost like a confidant, was a brawny individual with a red moustache. Myers Stultz was not in the posse. Then Chet remembered Jane speaking about a man called Red Barton whom Flint hired to work the adjoining claim. Maybe this was the man.

Ezra got down from the bay and grabbed the reins of his own horse. He succeeded in getting the saddle. And there he sat, looking mighty glum. With guns all around, it was useless to try any fool play. It would be just asking for lead.

'Throw them guns o' yourn on to the ground,' rapped Sheriff Brisbane. 'Don't try anythin'. You know durned well it would be asking for trouble.'

Grimly, Chet obeyed. Ezra threw his Colts to the shale, too. Then the rifles from the saddle holsters followed. Sheriff Brisbane jigged his horse forward and got down and gathered the hardware. He handed the rifles to a man who wore a deputy badge.

'Yuh under arrest,' grated Sheriff Brisbane.

Flint Randall and the red-moustached man had watched in jeering silence. But Randall shouted his intervention:

'Let's find a tree an' string 'em up now!'

'Thet damned poster is a forgery!' shouted Chet. 'We ain't wanted men! We ain't never bin in Creektown, Arizona!'

'Yuh cain't talk to us like thet!' sneered Flint Randall. 'The sheriff jest got those posters from the Town Marshal of Denver. Yuh're wanted men all right. I say string 'em up. What d'yuh men say?'

Before anything could be made of the growls, Sheriff Brisbane roared: 'These men are goin' back to the hoosegow! I reckon to clap 'em in jail. I'm the sheriff, an' what I say goes.'

The deputy sheriff nodded his agreement with this and some of the other men seemed to agree. This seemingly did not suit Flint Randall, for he glared at the sheriff.

As for Chet, he was undoubtedly surprised. What had motivated Sheriff Brisbane?

On one hand the sheriff had worked hand-in-glove with Flint Randall in order to have the false

'Wanted' poster printed and tacked up; and now he was announcing that Chet and Ezra should be taken to jail. Sheriff Brisbane knew that, given time, the two men could beat the charge. A communication need only be sent to the sheriff of Creektown, Arizona, in order to clear the men.

'I'm all fer stringin' these road agents up,' grated Flint Randall. 'Yuh got to show thet Devil's Fork ain't no hideout fer gunslingers.'

'Yep. A necktie party shore would suit these *hombres*!' shouted Red Barton.

'I'm stickin' these men in the hoosegow,' growled Sheriff Tom Brisbane. He looked challengingly at his deputy and three other men who were citizens of Devil's Fork. 'I'm the sheriff, an' what I say goes. Thet right?'

'Shore, thet's right with me!' snapped one man.

'Yep,' grunted the deputy.

The other men nodded.

'All right. Let's git ridin' back,' said Sheriff Brisbane grimly.

The party began the ride back to town. Ezra was on the roan, which was quieter now. But Chet and Ezra were minus their guns now. They had no chance to start anything. And in any case, as Chet guessed, that would have presented a first-class opportunity to Flint Randall for some neat gunplay.

But the ride back to town was very uneventful. As the trail skirted the Bennett mine and the cotton-woods lying about one mile distant, Chet thought of

Jane. It suddenly struck him; surely she would not believe the 'Wanted' posters?

He was trying to plan some ideas. One thing was sure: Flint Randall and the sheriff would not allow them to contact the sheriff of Creektown, Arizona. That would blow the frame sky-high.

Sheriff Brisbane's actions still puzzled Chet. The man was in Flint Randall's pay, although this theory might be difficult to prove at the moment. It was actually to his advantage to have the prisoners 'accidentally' killed. Yet he had gone out of his way to insist that they should be clapped in the jail.

Grimly, Chet Duncan decided there was only one thing for him to do at the moment, and that was keep mighty alert for the chance to clear his and Ezra's name. That and freedom.

They rode down the main stem of Devil's Fork accompanied by many curious glances from loungers on the boardwalks and saloon verandahs. Then the party dismounted at the sheriff's office. Chet and Ezra were led to the stone hoosegow at the back of the office and put in the cell. The horses were taken into the livery at the sheriff's office.

There was some argument among the men, but the words were muffled to the prisoners' ears. Then the men apparently dispersed.

Chet walked around the solid jail. He stared at the solitary barred window which looked out on to an alley between store buildings. The barred door of the cell gave access to the sheriff's office. Outside the door was a passage; then a door leading to Sheriff Tom Brisbane's office.

'Mighty comfortable,' was Chet's verdict. 'How long do we stick hyar?'

Ezra fumbled in his flapping vest for the makings of a cigarette.

'Shore wish I had thet bottle,' he groused. 'Say, this ain't right. We ain't wanted men by no durned sheriff. Why we was bounty hunters down in Arizony, remember?'

'I could bust this charge wide open if I had the chance to contact thet Creektown sheriff,' said Chet grimly. 'All we need is a friend to send a message through by the railroad telegraph. Thet's the quickest way.'

'Don't understand thet new-fangled telegraph,' grunted Ezra. 'Me – I'd git a fast rider. But thar ain't no justice when a town has a crooked sheriff.'

'Flint Randall ain't satisfied with this setup,' returned Chet. He walked to the barred door, stared into the empty passage. 'He wants us dead. Yuh know why?'

'I got idees. But yuh kin talk.'

'I told him we aimed to work the Bennett mine. Thet *hombre* don't like thet idee. He figgers to git rid o' us. I guess he wanted us strung up out thar in the desert. Dead men cain't contact sheriffs. Once we were in boothill the whole thing would be forgotten.'

Ezra struck a match to his cigarette and drew smoke from the brown-paper weed. He ran a grimy hand around his neck where a dusty red bandana hung.

'Cain't say I likes the set-up,' he muttered. 'I kin kinda feel the rawhide on my neck!'

'Yuh old grouse!' roared Chet. 'We ain't finished yet! I'll figger a way out o' this! I've saved yore old hide afore, an' I kin do it again!'

Ezra Blain grinned back. He really enjoyed his backchat with his young sidekick.

But the next few hours were dreary. They were only relieved when the deputy brought them some grub. He was very careful as he entered the cell. He had a gun in one hand and the tray in the other.

'Howdy, podner,' greeted Chet. 'Say, when do we git a chance to talk to Sheriff Brisbane about a lawyer?' The tall, lean man set the tray down.

'I'm Fred Newton, if yuh want to know. I cain't say what Tom Brisbane got in mind. Mebbe yuh'll git a lawyer.'

'Mebbe?' shouted Ezra. 'Why, hell, we're doggone entitled to a lawyer!'

'Wal, I figger yuh'll git one,' said the man.

'Those durned posters are a frame!' snapped Chet. 'Ain't no one around hyar goin' to believe us?'

Fred Newton hesitated. Then: 'I don't know anything about yuh two rannigans except what it says on them posters. Tom Brisbane gits his posters from the marshal – in Denver. Guess I'll talk the deal over wi' Tom.'

And then the deputy withdrew and carefully

locked the cell door.

'Thet jigger seems kinda puzzled about some-thin',' snapped Chet, when the man had gone. 'Maybe he ain't in Flint Randall's pay.'

The day wore on and the sun went down on the world outside. The cell became dark and full of shadows. Then, when sundown had given way to full night, Chet and Ezra found themselves in total blackness. In the main stem of the town lights spilled from the saloons and hotels, but the alley outside the barred window was absolutely dark.

There had been no sign of Sheriff Tom Brisbane all day. Chet felt really puzzled about the man. Why had he brought them back to the town jail if he did not intend to let them see a lawyer or make some preparation for their legal defence? Did he figure to keep them locked up from now on? If so, folks in town would talk. Even the sheriff could not do as he liked. There were law-abiding elements in Devil's Fork just as there were those who hated law because it got in the way of their ambitions.

Even Chet Duncan's grin vanished as they lay on the straw-filled bunks and the darkness deepened. Their plight was bad enough, but what of Jane? Surely Flint Randall would not resort to murder? He wanted to run the girl off the claim, but could he get away with murder? He had gotten away with it in the case of her father.

They were sitting very quiet in the black gloom, each man to his own thoughts. Chet was smoking the last of his tobacco.

He fancied he heard a sudden scraping sound at the barred window which looked out on the alley.

He stiffened, listened for more sounds. Maybe it was his imagination. Maybe he was getting jumpy. He was not usually nervy, but this tomb-like cell was not exactly the Grand Hotel.

All at once a gun roared and spat red flame. The slug hissed inches from Chet's face. He almost felt the heat from it as it passed.

He dived from the bunk and flattened against the wall at an angle which would make the gunman outside in the alley have a difficult job to aim. Ezra had followed with the same lightning reaction.

It was as well they had leaped, for the Colt roared again. The concussion in the cell was deafening. Flame lanced from the barred window overlooking the alley. The slug bit into Chet's bunk.

He gritted his teeth in helpless anger. He wished he had a gun in his hand. But the man outside probably knew they were without weapons. Someone wanted them dead. It was not hard to guess who that someone was!

There was sound of a man coming into the passage leading to the cell door. Swiftly, Sheriff Brisbane appeared, gun in hand.

Before he could open the door, Tom Brisbane sensed the movement of the gun at the barred window. *Crack*!

The sheriff's Colt roared. The slug whammed to

66

the window, scraping dust off the stone blocks.

Chet hugged the wall grimly. He saw Ezra on the other side of the cell trying to look like a shadow. Then Sheriff Brisbane ran back to his office door.

A few seconds later Chet heard sounds in the alley as two men stamped around, evidently searching for the gunslinger. But there was no doubt the man had made off.

Chet drew a deep breath.

'Yuh kin relax, old-timer,' he said. 'Thet jigger had his chance an' missed.'

'Durn yallerbelly!' snarled Ezra. 'Iffen I'd had me gun, I'd ha' blasted his durned eyes!'

'Thet gink knew we were unarmed,' returned Chet.

'Blamed snakeroo!' cursed Ezra. 'Did yuh see him?'

'Nope. But I kin guess it was Randall – or one o' his rannigans!'

'I figger it was one o' Randall's hellions!' roared Ezra. 'Thet gent uses his gold to buy gunmen!'

A minute later Sheriff Brisbane appeared at the cell door. Behind him was Fred Newton, the deputy.

'Yuh two all right?' barked the sheriff.

'We got nerves!' drawled Chet.

'Yep. We don't like this place!' snapped Ezra.

'We kinda long fer the open spaces. When do we see a lawyer, Mister Sheriff?'

'Mebbe all the lawyers in this town are as crooked as the sheriffs!' goaded Chet.

'Yuh kin turn off thet blastit talk,' grated Tom Brisbane.

'When do we git a chance to defend ourselves?' rapped Chet.

'Yuh'll git a chance.'

'Yeah? Why the hell didn't yuh let thet *hombre* have another blast at us? Shore would ha' saved yuh some trouble.'

'Thar won't be no more shootin!' said Sheriff Brisbane harshly.

'How d'yuh aim to stop it?'

'Jest shut yore trap. Thar won't be any more shootin'.'

And with that the sheriff withdrew.

Chet had the feeling of being like a rat in a trap. He saw no reason to believe the sheriff. The man had conspired to frame him.

There was the long night to pass. Chet could not see himself getting much sleep. The gunny could slink up again in the alley and trigger off some more shots. Unless Sheriff Tom Brisbane really had some way of preventing this.

For the next hour, the two prisoners maintained a grim vigil. They stared at the barred window, seeing the slightly lighter shade of darkness.

Then there was a sound at the cell door again. Chet and Ezra wheeled as one man.

They saw a figure standing in the gloom. The man held a gun.

'All right!' Chet drew a deep breath. 'Get it over, man!'

'Listen closely,' grated the man in a muffled sort of

voice. 'I'm lettin' yuh out. Don't try any clever tricks. Jest do as I tell yuh.'

'Yuh lettin' us out!' repeated Chet, amazed. 'Who the devil are yuh?'

'Never mind that. I've got the key. Yuh'll find yore hosses in the alley. They're saddled an' there's a grubstake. Light out o' this territory, *hombres*. Come back an' yuh'll git kilt.'

Chet took a few steps to the cell door. He soon discovered that the man was masked with a red bandana over the lower part of his face. With the Stetson low over his eyes, it was impossible to identify the man.

The man put the key in the lock, then paused. 'Yuh promise to try no tricks?'

'Yuh're doin' the talkin',' retorted Chet. 'All right, feller, we promise. Jest let us out o' hyar.'

'Promise to light out o' this town?'

'We cain't say thet,' snapped Chet. The man hesitated.

'All right, durn yuh. Yuh gittin' a chance. It's on yore own head!' he snarled.

He unlocked the door. Chet walked out, followed by Ezra. Chet passed close to the man, stared at the gun. 'Let's git to them hosses,' snapped Chet.

They went down the passage to a door. The man opened it and motioned them to step out.

Chet obeyed with wariness tingling all his senses. He was ready for a trap. Right now he trusted no man.

The door gave on to the side of the sheriff's office. A few steps and they were round in the alley. Standing in the gloom were two horses. As Chet and Ezra came closer, they saw the familiar outlines of the roan and bay.

Another second and they climbed to saddle leather. Chet paused, leaning on the saddle horn.

'Jest who are yuh, feller?'

'Forget it.'

'Why do this for us?'

'Quit askin' questions. Git goin'.'

Again the voice was muffled. Chet tried again.

'What about our guns? Kin yuh git us our guns?' The man hesitated.

'All right. A *hombre* is entitled to his guns. Jest don't move. I'll be right back.'

And a few seconds later the man returned from the sheriff's office and handed Colts to Chet and Ezra.

Chet stuck his promptly in his holsters. Ezra examined his to see if they were still loaded.

'Wal, hit the trail, *hombres*. An' remember – yuh're on yore own from now on. Yuh got a chance.'

'Adios,' snapped Chet.

He jigged his bay forward, riding the animal slowly down the alley. The last he saw of the stranger was the dark shape standing close to the side of the clapboard office. Then Chet and Ezra were riding carefully down the back of the town's main stem. Here it was unlighted and dark. If they encountered anyone, they would pass unnoticed. They would be taken for just two more riders coming into town.

'Who was thet jigger?' asked Ezra.

'Thet gink was Sheriff Tom Brisbane,' said Chet calmly.

FIVE

They rode out of the town at a pretty fast pace as soon as they got away from the lights. Ezra began to sing an old Mex song.

'Yep,' observed Chet, 'Sheriff Tom Brisbane let us out o' the jail. Couldn't be any other feller. Ask yoreself – if it wasn't him, where was the sheriff?'

'Podner, I ain't askin' questions!' rejoined Ezra. 'I figger it's good to be out hyar in the night with a hoss an' a gun.'

'Sheriff Brisbane is playin' a queer game,' said Chet. 'I don't know how he's goin' to account fer us escapin' to Flint Randall. But this squares wi' him stoppin' Randall from stringin' us up. Tom Brisbane didn't want our deaths on his hands – that's the way I figger it.'

'Wal, so now we got to light out o' this territory!' commented Ezra.

'Like heck!' snapped Chet. 'We're ridin' to see Jane Bennet. She'll ha' heard the news about the false posters, an' I want to talk to her.'

73

'What happens next?'

'Mebbe we kin take things up wi' Flint Randall. We shore ain't ridin' away. Mebbe it will be on our head, but that's the way it is.'

Over the dark, arid land they rode and finally approached the cottonwoods that grew near to the Bennett mine. There was a light in the shack window. The two men rode closer and saw the half-finished work on the extension they had been building.

Chet dismounted and walked warily to the shack door. It was pretty grim that he should have to move around with the feeling that a trap always lay ahead.

He knocked on the door. A minute passed, and then Jane's voice called.

'Who is there?'

'It's Chet an' Ezra!' shouted the young rannigan. The door opened at once. Chet nearly walked into the girl's arms!

'I heard yuh were clapped in jail!' she cried. Chet grinned.

'Wal, we got released by a mysterious stranger! I reckon we cain't stay long, Jane, but I got to talk to yuh.'

She admitted them and closed the door and put the bar in place. Chet and Ezra sat down.

Jane Bennett was a girl with good old-fashioned ideas. Men needed something to eat and drink – especially when they had just got out of jail! She hurried to make them coffee. Luckily a pan was on the boil. And she had some freshly-baked pie. Ezra

Blain's eyes gleamed at the sight of the food.

'Thet's what I want! Thet prison chow don't suit a feller wi' my constitution!'

Chet began to eat and talk at the same time.

'We were framed,' he said quietly. 'I don't know what yuh heard, Jane, but yuh got my word we ain't robbers an' murderers. Them posters were printed by Flint Randall – or Sheriff Brisbane. But thet galoot is shore playin' a mighty queer game. I figger he let us out o' his hoosegow – after workin' to stick us in.'

And Chet told the girl everything, from the chase and the reason why they rode away from the mine that day only to be rounded up when Ezra's horse fell.

The girl listened intelligently, and Chet felt plenty of admiration for her. It was good to talk to a mighty fine girl; and it was good to eat her home-cooking!

'If Tom Brisbane let yuh out, he'll have to explain a lot to Flint Randall,' she commented. 'What will he say? Will he say yuh escaped?'

'Thet's his only alibi,' said Chet. 'Maybe he'll fake the jail to look like we bust out somehow. Randall will be mighty sore and suspicious. Yeah, I guess. Sheriff Brisbane is in Randall's pay, but all the same he stopped at having us killed.'

'But what will yuh do now?'

'We'll have to go into hiding for a few days,' said Chet quietly. 'But we'll be around. Flint Randall won't chase yuh off this property. One o' us – Ezra or me – will have to contact the sheriff of Creektown,

Arizony, an' get the proof to clear our names. Mebbe it 'ud be a good idee iffen we contacted the Town Marshal of Denver. Sheriff Brisbane is under his juris-diction.'

'Mighty fine words!' ejaculated Ezra in admira-tion.

'Git on with thet pie,' countered Chet. 'I went to school while yuh chased dogies.'

'Chasin' dogies is an eddycation,' began Ezra. 'Yuh won't be able to work the mine if yuh're in hiding!' cried the girl, in disappointment.

Chet's eyes gleamed.

'Now thet ain't quite right. I got an idee. We'll ride down hyar for sundown each night and work in thet drift at night. 'If one o' us is away, the other kin do the work. We don't want to waste any time seein' what makes this claim so mighty attractive to Flint Randall.'

'That's a fine idea!' Jane's red lips parted eagerly.

'Yeah. But I reckon it would be risky to start to night. I figger Randall might find out we ain't in the hoosegow an' start some night ridin'. So we got to mosey along, Jane. An' pronto!'

'Look after yourself,' she breathed.

He looked deep into brown eyes warm with some-thing more than friendship.

'I'll do thet,' he promised. 'Adios, Jane.'

She saw them to the door. 'Adios. Take care, Chet!'

'Durn tootin', I will!'

And then they were riding into the night. The obvious thing was to make for the hills. The hills were the time-honoured place for men on the run. And they were on the run. Tom Brisbane may have let them free in a secretive manner, but he might side with Flint Randall again if it came to another chase. It seemed to Chet that Sheriff Brisbane was in Randall's clutches. There could be no other explanation.

Chet was determined to find out what made the Bennett mine so important to Flint Randall. Working the drift at night was a good idea. But they would also have to clear their names. They could not be on the run all the time.

After three hours' riding, they reached the first foothills. The gullies and rocky outcrops afforded plenty of cover. They chose a natural hideout and ground-hitched the horses near some grass. As long as there was some grass, they would not stray.

'Wal, ain't the fust time I bin sleepin' out in the desert,' yapped Ezra.

He fumbled for the makings.

'We ain't hyar because we like it,' said Chet grimly. 'We're hyar because them hellions might figger to come lookin' for us.'

'Wal, we got Colts,' snapped Ezra.

'Yeah. But we didn't git them durned Winchesters back. Heck, those rifles cost plenty dinero!'

They bedded down for the night. The idea was Flint Randall and his cohorts could ride the hoofs off their horses, if they were looking for them, and still not find them in the hills.

But they were astir at early sun-up. Chet climbed a high outcrop to view the arid flatlands to the east, but he saw no sign of any riders. He came down again to find Ezra had made some breakfast with food from the grubstake given them when they had rode away from the jail.

'Wal, one o' us has to ride to clear our names,' declared Chet. 'I've figgered the best plan is to contact the marshal in Denver. If we could git him to ride into Devil's Fork, thet would blow the lid off Flint Randall's schemes. An' I'd tell the marshal thet jigger kilt Frank Bennett.'

'Guess we'll toss fer the job,' suggested Ezra.

Chet had a silver dollar and they used it. Ezra claimed the head. When the dollar finished rolling it showed head upwards.

'Yuh got the ride,' said Chet. 'Got it straight what yuh got to do?'

'Yep. See the Town Marshal and git the loop untangled,' said Ezra promptly.

'Keep out o' the saloons when yuh hit Denver.'

'Hell, I ain't the *hombre* to mix business wi' likker!'

'Git the saddle on thet hoss, amigo!' roared Chet. 'An' for Pete's sake, don't stop to throw lead if yuh sight any o' Randall's riders.'

'Mebbe yuh goin' to take it easy like while I ride the skin offen my rear!' bawled Ezra.

'Yuh an ornery old galoot. I shore don't know how

I put up wi' yuh all this time. If yuh want to know, I'm goin' to keep an eye on Jane Bennett.'

'Heh, heh, heh! Shore, yuh will! I kin see me bein' the best man at a weddin' afore lawng!' cackled Ezra.

He nearly got a kick in his pants for that crack.

'I got to watch Randall don't make another pasea at thet gal!' said the red-faced young rannigan.

'Shore wish I c'd meet a widder who 'ud take care o' me,' grumbled Ezra. 'I figger I ought to be married an' settled kinda.'

'Yuh should ha' bin married fifty years ago, yuh old hellion!'

'I wasn't born fifty years ago!' roared Ezra.

He nevertheless went to his roan and saddled the animal. He got some grub in the saddle-bag and fully loaded his Colts. Then he leaped to the saddle.

Chet got his bay ready for the ride. He saw the oldtimer through the foothills in the direction of Denver. Then, just before the oldster left him, he slapped him on the back.

'Adios. An' watch yore step, amigo.'

Ten minutes later Ezra Blain was a dark, small shape riding through the yellow, arid lands.

Chet Duncan rode out of the hills in the direction of Jane Bennett's mine. He realized he might be sticking his neck out, but he had to see the girl.

He rode warily across the plains but encountered no other riders. He cantered the horse up to the shack and dismounted.

He thought Jane might have come out to greet

him. But probably she was busy and had not seen his approach.

He walked up to the door and wondered why it was closed, seeing it was daytime. Perhaps the girl had gone away in the buckboard?

He knocked and the door swung in on its hinges. So it was not bolted from the inside. He called: 'Jane,' and received no reply.

He looked into the cabin and instantly his senses went taut.

The shack showed every sign of a struggle. A chair was overturned. A box had been swept to the floor and the contents spilled. The shotgun had been broken in half.

Chet needed no more than these signs to tell him that Jane had been engaged in a struggle. And he knew who had started the struggle.

Flint Randall had got at the girl – probably during the night or very early morning. It was pretty early even now. Where was Jane?

Chet swore terribly. If Flint Randall harmed a hair of the girl's head, he would have the man's hide for it! Chet cursed. He should have known better than to leave Jane even for the one night. Flint Randall had soon learned that his prisoners had got out of the jail.

He had struck another blow in taking Jane. But what use would this serve him? Did he intend to murder the girl in cold blood?

Chet Duncan went back to his horse and there was

no smile on his face. Instead his blue eyes blazed. His lean cheeks were taut. His firm mouth was thinned to a line.

He leaped to the saddle and rowelled the horse. He rode away at a fast lope.

He was going to see Flint Randall, and there would be Colt-fire unless he found Jane safe and sound.

It seemed Flint Randall was ruthlessly prodding the girl into quitting the mine. Maybe he intended to kill her, and maybe he figured to scare her away by making life unbearable.

Chet Duncan rode fast with a pounding of hoofs until he joined the trail to Devil's Fork. He burned up a mile of the trail and then left it and headed through a patch of land studded with cholla and saguaro cactus. Eventually, as he rode past the creek and the encampment of placer miners, he came within sight of Flint Randall's mine.

He reined his horse to a canter. Just to dash in was to ask for singing lead. With the 'Wanted' posters still tacked on the sheriff's office wall, the rannigans in Randall's pay would have every excuse for flinging slugs.

He would be lead-bait. That would not do Jane much good.

Suddenly luck was with him. He figured he needed a bit of luck. So far it had all been bad.

In the distance, a man rode out of the mining property. Chet was sure the man was the *hombre* with the red moustache. He recognized his build. He thought this man was Red Barton, whom Jane had referred to.

Red Barton was riding out alone as if he was going some place fast. Chet narrowed his eyes. Just what was this galoot doing?

Seeing the man gave him an idea. Maybe he was not Flint Randall, and therefore not the boss, but the man was heading away from the mining property and could be got at. If Flint Randall was in his home, it would be tough getting at the man.

Chet rode away from the mine before anyone spotted him. He cantered the horse through some sandy gullies, taking a track that would bring him around to the direction Red Barton was taking.

Ten minutes later he was behind an outcrop of rock waiting for Red Barton to pass by. He had seen the man coming along at a fair lope.

Chet drew both guns and sat silently on the bay. The horse was absolutely still. They were hidden from view of the man coming through the undulating terrain. The seconds ticked on and the tattoo of approaching hoofs became louder. Chet tensed. Guns stuck forward like twin cannons. He knew he had the drop on this man. He could blast him to eternity in a split second.

At the sound of the approaching horse's breath, Chet jigged his bay out. He used only a touch of the rowels.

'Raise 'em!' cracked Chet.

Red Barton's horse reared to a standstill. But as

the forelegs came down, the man had his hands high. He was no fool, and only a fool tried to beat drawn guns.

'Don't move or I'll blast yuh!' snapped Chet,

He jigged closer. The man eyed him narrowly. He was a brawny waddy with red hair under a flopping sombrero. Chet got close and leaned forward. He was around behind the man almost. He leaned forward and plucked the Colts out of the holsters. He noted they were shiny with use.

'Reckon we can talk now!' snapped Chet. 'Where's Randall got Jane Bennett?'

'I don't know what the hell yuh're talkin' about!'

'All right, feller. Git down offen thet hoss.'

The man paused sullenly.

'Why d'yuh want me off leather?' Chet raised the Colt.

'If yuh don't hit the ground, I'll put this slug into yore shoulder. Shore hurt like blazes.'

His finger curled around the trigger. The man got down swiftly enough.

Chet Duncan swung to the ground and approached the man. He stopped two yards from the fellow.

'Let's talk straight. Yuh're in Randall's pay an' yuh must know he's taken Jane Bennett off her mine last night. Where has he put her? I'm not askin' yuh what's his idee. I jest want to know where she is. Speak, durn yuh!'

'If yuh kill me, thet won't git yuh nowhere!' sneered the man.

Swift as a rattler striking, Chet rammed the gun into the man's face. The butt had swung forward with dazzling speed. Blood streaked down Red Barton's face where skin was scraped.

The man flinched and cursed.

His hands went to his empty holsters by sheer force of habit. But the guns were stuck in Chet's shirt.

'Talk, durn yuh!' gritted Chet. 'Or, by bech, I'll beat yuh to pulp!'

He made a feint with the gun. The man thought another blow was coming and he snarled incoherent words.

'All right. Speak up!' rapped Chet. 'I guess yuh know where Jane Bennett is. Jest give, *hombre*, or it will be too bad for yuh.'

'I was ridin' out to the cave!' snarled the man. 'Flint said I had to mount guard on the gal.'

'Yuh'll take me to this durn cave!' said Chet fiercely. 'Now. Pronto!'

He waved the man to mount his horse. Chet backed to his bay and swung to the saddle. He pointed a Colt at Red Barton. He holstered the other.

'Ride, feller. An' don't get tricky, or, by heck, I'll use yuh fer target practise an' trail this cave myself.' The man wiped his hand over his cheek, looked at the blood sullenly. He jigged his horse forward. Chet followed. After ten yards, he rapped: 'Git thet hoss into a canter, *hombre*!'

The man obeyed. He was a hard rannigan when he had the upper hand, but right now the cards were not stacked to his liking.

At a fair lope, the two riders headed for some broken country that preceded the distant hills.

Chet Duncan was burning inwardly. There was some grim satisfaction in knowing he was riding the trail to Jane's rescue, but he had an itch to tackle Flint Randall. He had one of his sidekicks on the end of a Colt, but that was not enough.

Chet wondered just exactly what sort of play Randall thought he was throwing. What was the idea of sticking the girl in a cave. No doubt she was a prisoner. What was Flint Randall's plan?

Red Barton led the way through a series of shallow gullies. The country was barren and lonely. Grimly, Chet watched the man. There was no chance for the *hombre* to try any tricky play.

And Red Barton knew all this. Out here in the arid land his life depended on playing straight with the man who held a gun at his back. A gun is a grim leveller.

All at once they came upon the cave. The mouth lay in the face of a red bluff known as a barranca. The way Red Barton rode his horse up to the cave told Chet that this was it. Then the man halted his horse. He sat in the saddle, grim and sullen.

'Yuh kin git down,' said Chet. 'Walk into thet cave an, by Gawd, don't try anything.'

'What the hell kin I try?' snarled the man.

Chet dismounted and followed the man into the cave. He walked steadily, boots crisp on the sandy bed of the cave. And then he saw Jane Bennett.

She was just lying propped against the side of the cave, with hands and feet tied with rope. Rage flooded Chet Duncan, and he had to control a desire to kill Red Barton out of hand.

He did push the man to one side. He took fast steps to the girl's side. Then, with a snarl, he ordered Red Barton to work at untying the ropes.

'Git them durn ropes offen this gal! Jane – are yuh all right? They ain't hurt yuh?'

'Oh, Chet, I'm all right – just scared a little. Why does Randall want to leave me here? Oh, Chet, get me away!'

'I'll git yuh away, honey. Don't worry.'

Red Barton had to free the girl. Under the menacing Colt, there was nothing else he could do. Soon Jane was able to stand. She had a little trouble with the circulation in her legs at first, but it passed. Chet supported her with one arm, while he held the hogleg grimly at Red Barton.

'Mebbe yuh know why Randall ordered this?' snapped Chet.

'I don't know nuthin'!'

'Yeah? Wal, I aim to find out. Sit down, Jane, while I take this jigger out an' make him talk.'

Under the impelling gun, Red Barton lurched out of the cave. Chet came after him. He suddenly whipped the gun over the man's head. It was a light, rasping blow, but it hurt.

'Thet ain't nothin' to what I might do if yuh don't talk!' snapped Chet. 'I guess yuh got a good idee why Flint Randall brought Jane up hyar. What is it?'

'All right, durn yuh!' Red Barton snarled. 'He stuck her here for the time being. He figgered to have her taken away – a helluva long way off. An' he figgered she would not be comin' back. Thar's a law about mine claims. They got to be worked. If a claim ain't worked for a year, the title lapses. Any gink can file claim then.'

Chet drew a deep breath.

'Thet low skunk figgered to send Jane away to some durned place for a year! I get it. Jest so he could step in and claim her mine! Shore plannin' a good way ahead! The goldarn snake! All right – what makes the Bennett mine so highly important to Randall?'

'Thet's one thing he don't tell anyone!' snarled Red Barton. He rubbed his head where Chet had struck him.

Chet watched him grimly. Something told him the man was speaking the truth. Flint Randall was shrewd and would trust few men with vital secrets. He bought his underlings' services, and they knew a certain amount, but that did not include the important secret.

'Yuh helped Randall work thet claim next to the Bennett mine,' snapped Chet. 'How much gold does Randall git out o' thet claim?'

'It's jest poor quality ore,' rapped Red Barton. 'Why does he hang on to it?'

'I tell yuh, I don't know. I bin down thet drift an' it ain't worth the workin'. Flint stopped digging some time ago. He stopped us all from workin' the claim. Nobody goes into the durned mine now.'

There was a convincing ring about the statements. Chet accepted the remarks. But it was puzzling. He had a hunch the adjoining claim to the Bennett mine meant something important to Flint Randall, but if this was so, it could not be the gold brought out of it. But what else could there be?

At that moment, Chet Duncan got a sudden idea. He realized he would like to examine Flint Randall's gold claim. Maybe he would find something. And maybe he would not. But he figured he would sure like to look.

'Git back into thet cave, *hombre*,' snapped Chet. Sullenly, the man stamped back. Jane got up as they entered. She avoided the man. She did not get in the line of Chet's gun either. Jane Bennett knew something about guns and the way men held them.

'Yuh kin have the pleasure of tying this jigger,' said Chet to the girl, and a slow grin came back to his lean face. 'He was sent up hyar to guard yuh. So I don't want him ridin' back to Randall.'

'Yuh cain't leave me tied!' rasped the man.

'Yore boss left a gal hyar!' rapped Chet. 'Don't make any fool play. Mebbe I ought to plug yuh instead!'

The remark just scared the rannigan. He was pretty sullen, but he made no move while Jane tied his hands behind his back. When that was done, Chet pushed the man down and finished the binding of the rannigan's feet.

'Thet's mighty fine,' observed Chet. 'Have a good time, feller. Guess we'll ride, Jane. Yuh kin have this snakeroo's hoss.'

Minutes later they were riding down from the gullies, taking a path through the winding outcrops and shale slopes. Cholla and ocotillo cactus grew profusely in the arid patches of soil. The heat rose from the rocks, enough to fry an egg. Jane was a lithe figure in red shirt and blue jeans tucked into riding boots. She looked more like a slim youth than a girl. Under a fawn Stetson, brown hair was coiled.

She told Chet how Flint Randall and Red Barton had arrived at her shack just before sun-up. They had watched, and when she had dressed and opened the door they made a pounce on her. They rode her up to the cave on Flint Randall's horse.

Chet gave an account of how Ezra Blain was riding away to Denver in an attempt to clear them of the 'Wanted' charge.

'When thet old *hombre* gits back, we'll be cleared,' said Chet. 'Mebbe he'll bring the Marshal o' Denver ridin' back with him. Nobody can fool the Town Marshal o' Denver City.'

'Randall made some remark about yuh breakin' jail last night,' said the girl. 'Said he didn't know how yuh had done it, but he was tellin' folks in Devil's Fork to shoot if they saw yuh.'

'Sheriff Brisbane must have covered up for himself,' commented Chet.

'Oh, how I hate all this fightin'!' cried the girl. 'Why cain't Randall leave us alone?'

'Something about yore mine stirs his greed,' said Chet. 'Must be a lode somewhere – but how the heck does Flint Randall know thet?'

'I don't understand it!' cried Jane.

'If we could git a chance to mine further along thet vein, we might learn somethin',' said Chet. 'Wal, I got idees on thet score.'

He kept a wary watch as they rode down from the foothills and made across the plain towards the mine. He was thinking about Red Barton's remarks. The man had said Randall did not work the adjoining claim to Jane's mine.

Chet figured he might take a looksee in to the mine! They got back to the shack without coming across any other riders. Jane began to tidy up. Chet watched, fascinated by the trim figure she made.

'Jane —' he began, and then stopped, red-faced.

She paused in her work, and smiled at him. 'Yes?'

'I wanted to ask yuh somethin',' he mumbled.

'Wal, Chet, here I am. What's on yore mind?'

Chet Duncan gulped. If he suddenly blurted out everything in his mind, Jane Bennett might be surprised. 'I kinda figger you an' me might – might go to a dance in the Church hall at Devil's Fork,' he said with a rush. Then he added: 'Thet's when me an' Ezra git cleared o' thet false charge.'

'Why, Chet, I'd love that!'

'Mebbe after we git dancin' we could – ah – er – talk about other things apart from Randall an' gold!'

'Why, Chet Duncan, I think I know what yuh mean!'

'Do yuh?' he gulped.

Suddenly he thought he was going too fast. He sure knew how to handle men and horses, but women were different.

All at once he muttered something and went out of the shack.

Jane Bennett stood with a soft light in her brown eyes. Her thoughts were happy and free. She was making discoveries about Chet Duncan.

Chet Duncan strode over the sand and shale and approached Flint Randall's mine.

There was no one around. There was no one to stop him taking a look into the claim.

The mine was a drift, like Jane's claim. The shaft went into the sloping ground and seemed to run towards the Bennett mine.

Chet Duncan walked into the mouth of the drift. He eased a gun out of the holster just in case. He stopped to listen. There was no sound. Had any man been down the drift, sounds would have come up.

He walked in until the light darkened. Then he moved very carefully and struck some matches. The drift went along for a considerable distance. The floor sloped all the time.

All at once the blank end was reached. Chet struck another match and paused to examine the walls and roof for a sign of a vein similar to the one in Jane's claim.

There was some sign of gold-bearing quartz, but it was slight and scattered. There was nothing here to justify the expense of mining the tunnel.

Suddenly a curious slab of rock met Chet's gaze. He bent down to examine it. The slab was perfectly formed and there were curious symbols carved into it. Swiftly, he realised it was Indian work. It was pretty old. Why was it here, and what did it represent?

SIX

Chet Duncan thought it was durned odd finding the slab of rock down a tunnel. The symbols reminded him of the old Indian remains he had seen in many of the ancient, long-dead cave-cities. There was a place in the Valley of Ghosts where an Indian civilisation had flourished long before the advent of the white man.

It struck him that the slab of rock with the carved symbols was not in the shaft by sheer chance. The slab had some meaning, some connection with Flint Randall's nefarious activities. But what?

The match went out. He struck another – his last.

He examined further the blank end of the mine. So far as he could determine, there was only rock and red soil and, roof-high, the thin scattering of gold quartz.

Chet searched around until the last match was dead. He knew he would have to return back to daylight.

He turned around. He could not see the end of the drift, for the working turned slightly. He was in complete darkness. He moved forward slowly, feeling his way with outstretched hands.

He progressed for some yards and then hairs on the back of his neck tingled!

He halted abruptly. He held his breath, listened. Ahead, scraping sounds told him someone was moving along the tunnel. He heard the crunch of boots on loose shale. He even heard the heavy breathing as a man tramped along.

Chet hardly knew how he had received the warning. It had been a sort of sixth sense in operation. For a second he had thought he had developed a fanciful imagination.

But the unknown man was real enough!

A sudden splutter sounded as the man struck a match. A glimmer of yellow light showed round the bend in the tunnel. The footsteps came on. The glow of light increased.

Chet edged flat against the tunnel wall. The next moment the match faded out.

It was then that Chet moved.

He realized the man might be Flint Randall or Myers Stultz or some unknown rannigan. Wal, he would tackle him!

He flung himself forward in the darkness. Boots dug at loose rock debris. There was a momentary warning to the unknown man as Chet flung on. Then the two men collided.

94

Chet Duncan had a terrific desire to punish some-body for the treatment of Jane Bennett. He figured this was a chance. He was a red-blooded young ranni-gan, and he figured he would hand out a good hiding.

Chet whipped pounding fists into the unknown's body a second after they met. Iron-hard knotted firsts dug deep and wickedly into the man.

And then the stranger retaliated. Fists like sand-bags on whipping saplings rammed at Chet.

In the dark, there was no chance to dodge blows. Chet took the ramming fists in the chest. He grunted deeply. Chet rammed more thudding blows at the man before him. It was like pounding a tree bole. But each blow hacked gasps from the man. Chet felt hot breath in his face. Chet twisted, tried to smash his fists through the other's weaving arms. As he moved, he got at the man from another angle.

The young rannigan slammed away as if bent on smashing his way through rock. Fists never stopped thudding and probing. He took the other's blows because there was nothing else for it. It was a slog-ging match. And somebody had to win.

The tunnel was filled with animalish grunts. The men fought with savage desperation. There was no give or relenting. Chet's opponent hacked with boots as well as fists.

The two men thudded from one side of the cave to the other. Trickles of rocky debris fell from the roof of the tunnel. Chet gritted his teeth as once he was slammed hard against the rocky wall. Then he surged in again, always sensing the position of the other man.

It was a grim, terrible fight in the utter darkness. The end was a long time in coming. Chet thought he was wearing the other man down. The man's punches lost some steam. He hacked for breath. He was moving backwards.

Chet slammed savagely, grimly. He felt the sticky blood on his fists. Blood was trickling into his own mouth.

All at once the other man stumbled. It was not an accident. He had gone down under a flurry of blows.

Swift as lightning, Chet moved closer. He bent down to the man with the intention of heaving him up and smashing him down again.

Desperate hands clawed for Chet's throat as the young rannigan got closer. The man got a grip – a grip furious with desperation. Chet tried to wrench the hands away. They were grim bands of iron. Chet felt his breath choke off as the man gripped and gripped.

Savagely, Chet fought and had to retaliate in the same manner. His hands slid to the other's throat. He got a terrible grip in seconds. He began to squeeze and attempt to wrench himself just beyond the other's reach.

After some grim seconds, his plan began to succeed. The other's hands slipped, gouging deeply into Chet's neck as they did so. Chet tightened his hold. It was a question of the survival of the fittest. There was death in the black tunnel.

The man hacked some terrible sounds from his strangled throat. Chet got a knee on the rannigan's chest, and he held him down grimly. The man's hands clawed wildly, seeking a grip. Then they began to gouge at Chet's wrists.

Chet knew he would have to kill this man.

He went on with the grim, grisly task. He wished now he had started shooting. At least it was a quick end.

Horrible sounds issued from the dying man's throat. The weaving hands tightened on Chet's relentless fists. The grip was maintained, and then slowly the man's hands slipped as unconsciousness overtook him.

Grimly, Chet Duncan maintained the pressure. After a minute he knew the man was dead.

Chet staggered up, to his feet. He leaned dazedly against the cave wall. Reaction was setting in. But he mastered the queer feeling. He wiped sweat and blood from his face.

Then he bent down and hauled the man up. The man was a lifeless dummy. He was dead, sure enough.

Chet hauled him along the tunnel. After tramping down the shaft, daylight appeared. He took a glance at the man.

It was Myers Stultz!

There was grim disappointment insofar that the

dead man was not Flint Randall. But, all the same, this was one enemy less.

Chet dropped the body back. There was nothing now but to get out of the mine. He figured to leave the body for Randall to discover. Maybe it might serve as a warning.

Chet Duncan was not sorry about killing the man. The fellow was a killer, and he had met a just if terrible end. Chet was sorry only in the fact that he had had to do the job. He had not liked it.

He walked out of the mine and was glad of the clear sunlight. He squinted into the light. It was good to be alive! He had escaped death!

Looking down at his garb, he realized he needed a clean-up. Jane Bennett would be startled to see him. But he had to return to the shack. For one thing, his horse was hitched to the rail outside.

He lurched up to the shack. Jane saw him approach. She was looking out of the window.

She came tearing out.

'What on earth is wrong, Chet? What's happened?'

'I had to kill a man,' he said grimly.

She gave a startled gasp. 'Where? How?'

'In Randall's mine. The *hombre* was Myers Stultz an' he's plumb dead now.'

'Yuh went down Randall's drift?'

'Yeah. I got somethin' to tell yuh – somethin' I found. But I guess I need a clean-up first. Heck, I must look pretty awful.'

Chet Duncan could not forget he was standing in

front of a mighty pretty girl!

'There's blood all over yore face,' cried Jane. 'Yuh'll have to let me clean it off.'

Chet managed a grin again.

'Shore, Miss Jane. I'll leave it to yuh.'

For the next few minutes questions were put to one side as she cleaned his face with cold water. There was a well in the yard in front of the shack. Frank Bennett had dug the well and had hit a spring deep down in the stratas of rock.

Finally, when Chet was presentable again and dust and blood was gone, she asked: 'What did yuh find in Randall's mine, Chet?'

'An old slab of rock with Injun signs cut on it.'

'Indian? I don't understand!'

'No more I. How come this slab is down thet mine? I don't git it, but thar's something connecting it with Randall's aim to git yore mine. Did yore father ever find trace of Indian remains around hyar?'

'If he did, he never mentioned it to me. I've always thought it was just desert land.'

'Shore is. But some old Injun towns were built in queer places an' then got covered with sand and shale over the centuries. Yep, it's mighty interestin', but I don't git the connection.'

'Yuh're talking of the old tribes who built towns?'

'Yeah. Not all Injuns roamed the plains.'

'I wonder why Myers Stultz went down the mine?' Chet laughed grimly.

'Mebbe we'll never know thet. He ain't goin' to tell

any jigger. Maybe Flint Randall sent him.'

'Even so, why did Randall send him?' she persisted. Chet shook his head.

'Cain't say. If there is a secret, Randall is keepin' it to himself, an' I guess iffen he sent Myers Stultz it wasn't a very important task.'

Some time later, Chet Duncan went out and stared reflectively at Jane's mine. Why was Flint Randall so interested?

He walked into the drift and took a lighted lantern. He found a pick at the blank end of the tunnel. He began work and cleared a few more yards of rock and debris.

Suddenly he heard shouts from Jane Bennett.

Chet dropped the pick and ran back along the drift. He got to the mouth and saw Jane beckoning hurriedly. 'Some riders are comin', Chet!'

He rushed out with long strides and stared over the yellow land. Sure enough, on the horizon were a number of riders with the tell-tale cloud of dust in the air. He could not as yet make out who the riders were. But one thing was certain: they were riding for the Bennett mine.

'Have to git out o' hyar, Jane!' shouted Chet.

He was still a wanted man. He had not to forget that point. Stopping to argue with the unknown men might be a chancy business. They might not believe his arguments.

He swung sharply to the girl.

'Have yuh got any friends in Devil's Fork, Jane? I

don't like the idee o' yuh stayin' out hyar alone. I cain't stick hyar all the time – not until Ezra git's back an' clears our names. If yuh have friends, maybe yuh could stay with them – mebbe for a night or so.'

The girl hesitated; yet it was a time for quick decisions. Chet was already getting to his bay.

'I don't really want to leave the shack an' mine,' she said. 'But I guess yuh got the right idea, Chet. I'll take the buckboard into town an' stay with friends for the day an' night.'

'Fine.' He jumped to the saddle. He looked down gravely. 'I'll be around, Jane. Don't yuh worry none about thet. I figger we kin beat Randall yet. *Adios!*' And with that he applied spurs to the bay and galloped out of the yard.

He let the horse go full out. Wide-eyed, the bay thundered over the arid plain. Hoofs spurted sand and chips into the air. He was on a fast ride to the foothills.

Meanwhile the bunch of riders thundered into the yard around Jane's shack. Horses reined in so abruptly that several of the animals were pulled back almost on to their haunches. But not one of the riders dismounted.

Leading the bunch were Flint Randall and Sheriff Brisbane. Behind the sheriff was Fred Newton, the deputy. Three other men made up the posse. Flint Randall stared jeeringly at Jane.

'We got word thet jigger Chet Duncan bin around

101

hyar. Was seen cuttin' down from the hills. My, but yuh lookin' purty healthy, Miss Jane!'

It was a sneer directed at the fact that she was no longer a captive in the cave. So Flint Randall knew Chet had rescued her! Someone had seen Chet riding down from the hills. Obviously there had been some delay in getting the word to Flint Randall – which was just as well.

At the moment, there was little Flint Randall could do to harm her because three of the possemen were townsfolk who knew that Jane Bennett had not offended the law. Even Flint Randall, with Sheriff Brisbane evidently in his power, had to watch his step with regard to the law-abiding element in Devil's Fork.

Jane stared contemptuously at Sheriff Brisbane. The man's weather-beaten features took on a grim look. Heaven only knew what his thoughts were.

'Let's hit the trail!' snapped Flint Randall. 'Thet blamed outlaw is makin' a getaway!'

'Guess it's a waste o' time now,' said Sheriff Tom Brisbane sullenly. 'He's got plumb away – an' thet bay shore got fast legs!'

'Shore is too bad we didn't git hyar a little earlier!' sneered Randall. His Indian black eyes flicked the sheriff. 'Wal, I guess yuh're right. Thet outlaw's got a headstart. Yuh kin take yore posse back to town, *hombre.*'

'I'll go with you men,' rapped Jane. 'I've been abducted by this snake once before. D'yuh know this man had me forcibly removed off my property,

102

Sheriff?' Flint Randall cut in with a bull voice.

'She's crazy. Kin she prove thet? Guess livin' out hyar alone is turnin' the gal's head. Shore is a pity. Mighty fine gal, too. Make a durn good wife fer some gink. But I figger she'd ha' to be handled like a bronc. Not a bad idee.'

Right through the sneering, insulting banter, Sheriff Brisbane was silent. But when Jane's eyes flicked him, he avoided her glance.

'Wal, we'll ride back,' said the sheriff harshly. That was all he had to say. It was just as if he had not heard Jane's accusation concerning Randall's plot to kidnap her.

But Fred Newton looked curiously at his boss. Still he made no comment. The three other possemen looked slightly puzzled, too.

Jane Bennett lost no time in putting her horse to the buckboard. She locked the shack door and climbed to the seat. Sheriff Brisbane nodded to the possemen and the whole party rode off.

Flint Randall rode only to the shack adjoining Jane's claim. He watched the possemen ride with the jolting buckboard into the distance, and the sneer on his lips was some indication of his thoughts.

Then he dismounted and walked casually to the mine. He stood for a minute and rolled a brown-paper cigarette. He lit the smoke, threw the match away and then walked into the mouth of the drift.

His whole actions were idle, as if he figured to take a casual look over his property.

He walked into the shaft and when the light gloomed as he progressed he struck a match.

The very first match showed the body of Myers Stultz lying in a grotesque sprawl.

Flint Randall dropped the burning match in his surprise. His breath hissed with sudden intake. He struck another match, bent over the body of his late sidekick.

He saw the obvious signs of the way the man had died. The sneer which had been stamped over Randall's lips twisted into something infinitely more ugly.

Flint Randall went on down the drift with a hunch of his shoulders. At the blank wall he struck another match. He looked down at the slab of rock.

He knew it had been moved. A crooked smile played over his thin lips. In the yellow light of the spluttering sulphur match, his Indian ancestry showed in his hawk-like cruel features.

As the match curled on the long stick, he started back for the mouth of the drift.

He was thinking about two men – Myers Stultz and Chet Duncan.

One was dead and anything he had learned had died with him. But the other was very much alive – and dangerous!

He did not give a hoot in Georgia for Myers Stultz and for a very good reason; he had not sent him to examine the mine.

But Chet Duncan was proving a dangerous *hombre*!

How much had he learned?

In the meantime, Jane Bennett rode into Devil's Fork and stopped her buckboard outside one of the prosperous stores. She climbed down and hurried round to the back of the store. A minute later she was admitted to the neat clapboard house at the back of the store, and was talking to her friend, Mrs Bryant.

'Could yuh let me stay with you a night, Mary? Oh, I've got lots to tell yuh! I guess yuh know Dad is dead. And Flint Randall is makin' trouble for me . . .'

Jane began to pour out her story to Mary Bryant. The storekeeper's wife had been a good friend for long enough.

'Shore, yuh can stay as long as yuh want,' declared Mrs Bryant. 'Huh, I've a good mind to speak to thet Tom Brisbane! The goin's on! This town ain't no better than an owl-hoot camp!'

'I've got a friend helpin' me,' said Jane, and she told the other all about Chet Duncan.

Flint Randall rode away from his claim adjoining the Bennett mine. He fed rowels to his horse and rode at a fast lope to his other and more prosperous mining property.

He hitched his horse to the tie-rail beside his home, and stamped off to the bunkhouse. He found Red Barton lounging and smoking. The man stared up with unspoken inquiries in his eyes when Flint Randall entered and sat close beside him on the wooden bench.

'Myers Stultz is dead,' said Randall softly.

Red Barton showed his broken teeth. 'How the hell . . .'

'Chet Duncan got him – killed him with his hands. Yuh ought to figger yoreself lucky, feller. Thet jigger could ha' killed yuh, too. Guess it would have served yuh right fer bein' so blamed careless in lettin' him git the drop on yuh.'

'How did I know thet hellion was waitin' fer me?' snarled Red Barton.

'Fergit it! Thet gal is figgerin' to stay with friends in town. Guess thet's the only reason why she left the mine. At the moment I cain't do anythin' about her. I figger to settle Chet Duncan – then the gal. Thet galoot rode into the hills. Guess he's hidin' thar with his segundo. Wal, I aim to smoke him out. Git yore hoss an' tell Al Sporn to git guns, hoss and saddle.'

'Yuh want me to ride with yuh after thet jigger?'

'Shore.'

'Guess Al Sporn will like thet,' muttered Red Barton. 'Thet feller likes ridin' an' shootin' better'n mining.'

'Thet's why I picked on him,' said Flint Randall, with a twisted smile.

They started on the ride some time later. They were three hell-bent rannigans and murder was just something in a day's work.

SEVEN

Chet Duncan rode for the foothills and cursed the feeling of being harried and hunted. He was not sure who the riders were, but he could not take chances. If they were possemen, he could not shoot it out. He was not an outlaw in the strict sense of the term. And he could not just idly walk into Randall's or Sheriff Brisbane's clutches.

Leaving Jane Bennett was not a pleasant feeling, either. He was putting a lot on trust. But the girl could not ride into the hills with him.

He had to play for time. Once Ezra Blain contacted the Town Marshal of Denver, the play would get untangled.

Chet halted the bay just before the land broke up into gullies and outcrops. He looked back, his keen blue eyes searching the horizon for the tell-tale cloud of dust. He sat tall in the saddle, looking back on his trail and realizing that the riders were not coming his way.

He rode to the nearest crag of rock and sat down in the shade and contemplated his next move. There was one thing; he hated being idle.

He figured he would rest the horse for some time and then ride back to Jane's mine. If no one was around, he might work on following the vein. There was some secret, and only work would unearth it.

For the next twenty minutes Chet was content to smoke and watch the bay nose for grass. There were a few patches of bunch grass growing where a little moisture could be extracted from the arid soil, but even this was browned with the sun. There was shade in the rock. Out on the plain the only shade a man could get was by sitting under his horse's belly!

Finally he realized that the hunt was not coming his way. There was no cloud of hoof dust on the horizon. Somehow he had shaken off the pursuit.

He got up and climbed to the saddle again. He got his water canteen and dribbled some on to the palm of his hand and held it to the horse's mouth. A raspy tongue licked his palm gratefully. Chet put the canteen back.

'All right, hoss, git goin'. Yuh cain't mosey around all day jest lookin' for grass. Ain't no grass around hyar anyhow thet's worth eatin' for a real cayuse.'

With a mere touch of the spurs, he jigged the animal on. They set off at a plodding walk over the arid plain again.

They had traversed a few miles, avoided an odd rattler sunning on baking rocks, when Chet suddenly noticed the small dust cloud away to the west. Wary at once, he halted the bay and watched keenly.

After a minute he knew the riders were heading for the foothills. But they were heading in a direction that would take them past him. They were a mile or more to one side and would not overtake him.

He got the horse to lie down, and he squatted down beside the animal. He waited some minutes and then rose to his feet to stare around. He located the slight suggestion of a dust cloud. It was far away. The riders were heading for the foothills.

Grimly, Chet wondered who the men were. He had a good idea it might be Flint Randall and his *hombres* or else the sheriff and a posse. But he could not help but think that Sheriff Brisbane would be reluctant to chase a framed man to any great extent.

The dust cloud slowly vanished, proving the riders were well to the west. There was no danger they would overtake him.

But Chet Duncan was not satisfied with that.

He was a red-blooded young rannigan and wanted action. He had a hunch the riders were looking for him. In that case, he would track them!

He urged the bay to a canter. He rode straight across the arid plain in the direction of the other men. Within fifteen minutes he had found the trail of the hard-riding *hombres*. He halted the bay, stared down at the hoof-prints.

Three riders! That was kinda interesting!

He rode slowly in the direction of the tracks.

They presented no trouble to follow. Even on the shale, there were signs which his expert eyes picked up. A loose bit of slate kicked to one side by a passing hoof was enough for Chet Duncan. He had learned his trailcraft from Indians, on the reservations, when a boy.

But the sign could not tell him the identity of the three men. That would remain to be seen. But he had his hunches and was prepared to follow them.

The ride soon led into the hilly country. He did not see the three riders. There was no sign of them, except the fresh trail which he followed.

The three riders did not separate. They stuck together. The hoof-prints were now in single file as the trail led through narrow gullies and defiles among the jagged rocks.

Chet jigged the bay slowly forward. At one time he stopped to consider whether to climb a high pinnacle of rock in order to sight the men.

As the horse stood motionless, his keen ears picked up sounds of hoofs on rock. Chet listened tensely. It suddenly struck him that he was not overtaking the riders. They were returning down the trail again.

Maybe they had rode into a blind position among the broken land. But the sounds seemed to indicate horses cantering down along the trail again.

Chet wheeled his bay and sent it climbing a steep shale slope. In minutes he was in hiding, behind a chunk of weatherbeaten rock as big as a shack. He

110

could look down on the narrow trail as it wound through the defile.

Listening to the tell-tale sounds, he realized it would be another second or two before the other riders cantered down.

Chet eased his Colts from leather. A taut grin was on his firm lips.

The way he figured it, the rannigans were looking for Ezra and him. As a rule there was nothing up here in these arid hills to attract men from Devil's Fork. Maybe a lone prospector would go into the hills, but a bunch of riders was another thing.

Seconds passed and then the three riders appeared around a rocky bluff.

Chet recognized Flint Randall and Red Barton. He did not know the third man, but he could be classified as Randall's hired ruffian, sure enough.

Chet drew a bead on Flint Randall. He did not like the extreme range, but he would have to take a chance. Something happened at that crucial second which was just the devil's own luck for Flint Randall.

One of the horses down in the defile suddenly whinnied.

The sound was sudden and swiftly meant only one thing to the horse-wise riders in the gully. The neighing horse had scented another!

Chet triggered his gun.

Crack!

But Flint Randall had spurred his animal almost simultaneously with the whinney from the horse.

Chet's slug hissed through the thin air an inch from the man.

Chet snapped another shot, but it was too quick and the range was pretty long.

The next second a rataplan of shots chipped rock all around him. Randall's *hombres* were shooting back! Chet had to duck because he figured to live for another day. All the same, he bobbed up twice and snapped slugs at the madly riding men. The *hombres* were firing back, guns in grim outstretched fists. They were wild, chance shots. But chance slugs sometimes found targets.

In another second the rannigans were behind cover. Chet could have laughed aloud. They had rode to hunt him down, and he had started the play by stampeding them into confusion.

Chet Duncan slid back from the edge of the rock and reached out for his horse. He was not fool enough to imagine he could play three gunslingers. Because the other three could surround him in time. If he stayed put that would be their scheme. But he was not staying!

Randall's rannigans were now behind rocky cover and probably planning to fan out.

Chet climbed to the saddle. He looked up the slope.

He figured he had a chance to ride away now. If he did not, the time would come when guns would roar at him from three different sides.

The bay sprang up the shale slope with hoofs that

sent rocky debris rolling. Four seconds after Chet urged the horse out of hiding, guns snapped slugs his way.

But the range was too far for accurate fire from Colts. The slugs whined like angry hornets, but they were wide of the mark. Another four seconds, and Chet had reached the ridge of shale and was sending the horse plunging down the other side.

He reached a gully that apparently led to other narrow passages among the heaped-up rocks. The bay sped along, twisting and taking the sharp corners like wind.

As the minutes passed, Chet figured he was making a good getaway. He laughed grimly when he thought of Flint Randall's anger. The galoot would be sore as a disturbed rattler.

Chet reached the floor of a small canyon and sped down the entire length, a crouching horseman on a flying steed. He threw a backwards glance and knew he had shaken off pursuit. He had lost Flint Randall and his hellions in the maze of jagged trails.

They could not see him, and his trail over the rocky land would be hard to find. They did not know whether he had gone north, south, east or west.

But riding down to Jane's mine was not too wise. It seemed that Flint Randall was hunting him.

Chet pondered over the possibility that Randall might be puzzled at lack of sign of Ezra Blain. But Randall might figure they had just separated temporarily. He would be dangerous if he guessed Ezra was riding to Denver.

Chet was suddenly impatient. It seemed that Randall was doing all the prodding.

On a sudden impulse, he spurred the bay to full gallop. To the devil with this waiting game! He figured to work on the mine. Maybe he would find what made it so important to Flint Randall! That was the key to the present situation – that and clearing their names of the false charges.

Wal, Ezra was riding to fix that job, so somebody ought to tackle the other!

Chet headed the horse back over the plains with a rapid tattoo of hoof-beats. For the next few miles he was just part of the galloping animal. Crouched low on the saddle, he gave the horse full head. The gallant bay simply tore up the miles.

The clump of cottonwoods and the rocky pile-up appeared in the distance. Chet tore up on the big bay and threw himself from the saddle. He approached the shack and saw the bolted door.

'Guess Jane went off to town!' he muttered. He saw the corral was empty. The buckboard had gone, too. So the girl had ridden off to town to stay with friends as he had advised. In that case, it seemed likely that the riders who had approached the mine had included Sheriff Brisbane. That *hombre*, although in Randall's pay, would not and could not harm Jane.

Chet hitched the horse to a tie-rail. There was water in a trough near the rail. With a pat on the bay's flanks, Chet walked over to the drift mouth.

He stood for a moment staring reflectively at the shaft.

'Heck, I wonder jest what there is in thet tunnel? Shore must be somethin' valuable. Must be gold. Wal, I don't figger how Randall know's there's a lode. If thet gink had dug towards a bonanza from his shaft, he'd ha' had the gold mined by now! No, sir! I don't git it!'

But Flint Randall, with the callousness of his ancestry mixed with the greed of his white blood, had killed Frank Bennett, goaded Jane and framed Chet and Ezra in an attempt to drive them from the property. He had even asked Jane to marry him! He had started on the idea of abducting the girl and taking her away to some distant place for a year so that title to the claim would lapse. He had been able to do most of this because he had Sheriff Brisbane in his power.

Chet went along the drift. He got a lantern and lighted the wick. Head down, he moved along the tunnel until he reached the face. He examined the vein of quartz and sighed. To his mind, there was nothing here to raise optimism. There was gold in the quartz, true. But it would need work to extract it. Without expensive plant, they would have to crush the ore by hand. Flint Randall had one of the new-fangled steam crushers at his other, more profitable, mine.

There was always the possibility that the vein would run into a lode of pure gold. Frank Bennett

115

must have had that in mind when he talked of his daughter's gold. Sure, optimism was a grand thing, but you could not sell it as gold.

Chet grabbed the pick and swung it. There was only one thing to do. The vein had to be followed until it ran into a lode or petered out. The vein might easily travel for many yards, and the shaft would have to be shored up as the excavation proceeded. Actually, the job would take a long time.

For half an hour, Chet worked steadily. He uncovered the vein for about another yard, and then had to start fixing a timber to support the roof. Staring at the vein, he decided there was no more gold present than at any other portion.

With the pick head, he tapped the timber baulk into position and then figured to make a cigarette.

He put the pick down.

He was quietly rolling the tobacco into the brown paper when he heard the sound of footsteps along the drift.

He threw the makings away, and a gun appeared magically in his hand.

He waited. The lantern threw a yellow gleam. The oncoming man must have known someone was present in the shaft. The man came on, confidently.

In seconds the bulk of the man appeared. He walked straight into the glow of light and stopped and stared at Chet Duncan and the grim gun.

'There ain't no need for thet hogleg,' said Fred Newton quietly.

'Yuh got a pair dangling in leather yoreself.'

'Shore. But I don't aim to touch 'em. I didn't expect to find any jigger hyar, but now thet I've found yuh, Duncan, mebbe we kin talk.'

'Shore. I'm a peaceful *hombre*. I'd sooner talk than anythin' else.'

'That's fine. What are yuh doin' hyar?'

'Lookin' for gold,' said Chet quietly. 'On Miss Jane's behalf. Matter o' fact, Jane an' Ezra Blain an' me are podners.'

'Kinda hard to work this gold, ain't it?' Fred Newton glanced at the walls of the drift.

'Guess it is. Kin I ask what yuh're doin' hyar?'

'Jest moseying around.'

Chet Duncan put his gun back to holster.

'All right, then let's talk, *hombre*. Yuh're Sheriff Brisbane's deputy. Yuh know he got out a poster fixing Ezra an' me as wanted men. Thet poster is a frame up.'

'I'm beginnin' to think yuh're right,' said Fred Newton coolly.

Chet's grin became more pronounced.

'Fine. Now Tom Brisbane is in Flint Randall's power. I don't know how. Mebbe he takes money from him – I don't know. But we cain't expect justice from Sheriff Brisbane.'

Fred Newton took a deep breath.

'I give yuh thet, Duncan. I've found out somethin'.'

'What?'

117

'Thet poster was printed in Devil's Fork. Tom Brisbane shore didn't git it from Denver. Unless a poster comes from the Town Marshal at Denver, it ain't got no authority.'

Chet gripped the other's arm.

'Thanks, *hombre*! Yuh're with us, then?'

'Maybe. I stand fer justice, thet's all.'

'Yuh're a man after my own heart. I'm a-goin' to tell yuh thet Ezra Blain is ridin' to Denver to contact the marshal. Soon as we git cleared, there'll be a day o' reckonin'. In a way, I'm sorry fer Tom Brisbane. He ain't as black as Flint Randall. Thet *hombre* kilt Frank Bennett. We found Frank Bennett an' he named Flint Randall an' Myers Stultz as his killers. But thar ain't no need to worry none about Stultz.'

'Why not?'

'He's dead,' said Chet quietly. 'I killed him. I left thet jigger's body in the claim next to this – Flint Randall's claim.'

'Was it self-defence?'

'Shore. I've never killed a man otherwise, except a few outlaws with a bounty on their heads!'

'Jane Bennett rode back to town wi' us,' said Fred Newton. 'I found out she's stayin' with Mrs Bryant, a storekeeper's wife. Mebbe yuh'll be glad to hear thet?'

'Shore am.'

'Another thing: Jane Bennett said Randall had abducted her. Yuh know anythin' about thet?'

'Yep. Randall figgered to take her away – a hell of

118

a long way off. He reckoned to keep her away from Devil's Fork an' the mine for a year. When the title lapsed, he figgered to step in an' claim the mine. But I happened to git Jane out o' the cave he had stuck her in kinda temp'rary.'

Fred Newton stared curiously at the mine walls. 'What makes this drift so mighty valuable to Flint Randall? I don't git the idee.'

'Mebbe the vein runs into a bonanza.'

'Yuh found sign o' a bonanza?'

'No sign,' admitted Chet. 'So far it's poor quality quartz – same as the other claim owned by Randall.'

'Why does thet *hombre* bother with thet claim?'

'Yuh askin' mightily pointed questions, Fred. Thar's only one answer. Randall thinks there's somethin' valuable to be found in this mine, an' he hangs on to the other claim because it links up somehow. The two drifts run towards each other. In time they could run into each other.'

Fred Newton crinkled his lean face.

'Shore is mighty interestin'. Wal, I believe most o' what yuh say, except thet yuh got to prove thet Randall kilt Frank Bennett.'

'Thet ain't easy,' muttered Chet. 'Thet hellion kin git witnesses to swear he weren't in the desert when Bennet was kilt. But right now we're workin' on clearin' our names an' findin' what is the secret o' this mine.'

'There ain't much I kin do until yore podner gits 'ord from the Town Marshal o' Denver,' said Fred

119

Newton. 'Goldarn it, I ain't happy about Tom Brisbane. He used to be a mighty fine feller.'

'He ain't too bad,' said Chet quietly. 'I kin tell yuh he let us free from the hoosegow the other night. He told us to git goin' an' light out o' town. But thet ain't the way Ezra an' me see it.'

'He let yuh out?' exclaimed Fred Newton. 'He told me yuh tricked him an' bust out. He had blood on his face an' the office was kinda knocked around.'

'A blind,' commented Chet. 'Mostly to fool Randall, I guess.'

'Wal, I'm goin',' grunted Fred Newton.

'Yuh goin' back to Devil's Fork?'

'Shore.'

'Take a message to Jane Bennett, will yuh?'

'Yeah, I'll do thet.'

'Tell her I'm one move ahead o' Flint Randall. Tell her I still got a whole hide.'

Fred Newton smiled.

'Ef thet's in the interest o' justice, I'll do it.'

'It's in the interest o' plenty of other things 'sides justice,' said Chet Duncan, with a wide grin.

The two men walked back along the drift. They came out into the sun and blinked a little in the light. 'Yuh podner cain't git back from Denver until late tomorrer,' commented the deputy. 'I'm sidin' with yuh an' the Town Marshal, but I'm mighty unhappy about Tom Brisbane.'

'The best thing he could do would be to ride out o' this state,' said Chet harshly.

'Yeah. Mebbe I'll give him the tip – when yore podner gits back safe an' sound.'

'Ezra will git back,' said Chet with conviction.

Chet saw the deputy ride away into the distance. Heat hazes drifted up on the horizon with a mirage-like effect. He turned around and stared reflectively at the mine. His little amount of work had brought him no nearer to getting the secret. He figured a whole heap of work was needed.

He scanned the horizon again, and it was as well that he did before entering the drift again.

For away to the west was a tell-tale cloud of dust. It was the dust that accompanied flying hoofs. Riders were on their way, and they might easily be heading for the shack and mine. A few more minutes would tell. Five minutes later, black shapes appeared out of the dust cloud. Riders were urging horses over the arid land. They seemed to be heading for the mine, too. 'Mebbe Randall and his hellions!' muttered Chet. 'But I'm durned if I aim to ride out!'

He led the horse to the shelter of the drift mouth. He ran back to the shack and shot back the bolts. He dashed inside. The first thing he saw was a rifle on the wall. He grabbed at it. He hunted around and found a box of shells in a locker. Apparently the gun had belonged to Frank Bennett. Jane had been more at home with the shotgun.

Chet waited until the dark shapes materialised into riders and horses. They were undoubtedly heading right for the shack.

As the seconds passed, he identified three riders. Then he knew Flint Randall with his two sidekicks had ridden down from the foothills after their abortive effort to find him. They figured to look over the mine, just in case. Wal, they were right in looking here for him!

But they would get as much as they figured to hand out! The rifle was better than a Colt for long distance shooting.

Ten minutes later, Flint Randall rode into range. Chet waited and then poked the rifle through the already broken window. He drew bead on the man.

It was a long shot, but he fired.

The steel-jacketed shell whined through the air and hit Flint Randall. The force of the shell nearly unseated the man.

But Chet's aim had been hurried for the long-distance shot. He saw Flint Randall lurch in the saddle and then clap a hand to his shoulder. Simultaneously, the man jabbed steel to his horse and bounded out of range.

The other two rannigans galloped after their boss. Chet sped them on their way with a volley of rifle fire, but the shells fell short.

Chet grinned to himself. He could see Randall was wounded. It seemed a shoulder hit, judging by the way the man held his hand up.

In the next few seconds the three riders rode away furiously.

EIGHT

Chet Duncan watched the three hellions ride off. He waited until he was sure they were not returning immediately. He guessed Flint Randall was more interested in a doctor now. There was only one doc in Devils' Fork, and that was Doc Wilson. Chet grinned. He had sent some business Doc Wilson's way!

For another hour Chet worked in the mine drift. He dug and shored. He uncovered another length of the vein of gold-bearing quartz. He cleared away the debris and heaped it to one side. By the aid of the lantern, he began to attack the face again with the pick when all at once he was struck by the curious markings on the rock in front of his face.

He stopped and examined the markings. He rubbed the smooth portion of rock with his hand and dust came away. It was the dust of old, dead rock.

Intrigued, he cleared all round the flat face with the pick. After a while, he had a large flat slab of rock laid bare, and on the rock were Indian signs and symbols.

He knew at once he had uncovered some part of an old, long-dead civilisation. The slab of rock was man high and solid. It was all one piece and not living rock.

He could make no sense of the symbols. They were beyond his knowledge. But the significance of this find was not lost on him.

This slab of stone was bigger than the one he had found in Flint Randall's mine, but it was undoubtedly similar.

Scaring at the mysterious slab, he knew it to be part of an ancient Indian site. Maybe there was a tomb ahead or an old building which had been covered with sand and shale during land upheavals over the centuries. If the remains were a vault, then they had deliberately been buried. Was this what Flint Randall sought?

Chet was staring at the strange slab, wondering if he could dig around it, when he heard a sudden sound at the mouth of the tunnel.

Chet whipped round. Guns flashed to his hands. A mocking voice echoed down.

'Yuh're a nosey *hombre*! Wal, we aim to fix yuh!'

Flint Randall's voice!

The man was undoubtedly a hard customer. He had taken a shoulder wound and then returned.

Chet started forward.

'Git out o' my way!' he roared. 'I'm a-comin' with guns!'

'Stay put!' mocked Flint Randall. 'Or we'll blast yuh. I got Red Barton with me an' Al Sporn. I bin fixed up by the doc. And I kin use a Colt with my right hand. Still figger to come out shootin', feller?'

Chet retained a thin smile on tight lips. He halted. It was justifiable.

He realized he would run right into a volley of Colt fire. They could fill him with lead. Soon as he became visible in the half-light, they would shoot.

Chet figured he might get one, but they would get him. That did not seem much of a deal. He hesitated.

'Yuh bin diggin' fer gold, feller?' rasped out Flint Randall.

Chet roared back.

'Yep! I found plenty – but not gold!'

'Yeah? Wal, thet's too bad. Yuh ain't gonna learn much more!'

Chet flattened against the tunnel wall.

'How come?' he bawled.

'Where's thet old side-kick o' yourn,' rasped Flint Randall. 'How come yuh're workin' solo?'

'We split,' snapped Chet.

'Yeah? What the blazes for?'

'He's in the hills.'

'Like hell he is. Jest what sort o' play are yuh makin', Duncan?'

'Guess yuh'll find out!' jeered Chet.

'Wal, as a matter o' fact, we kin take care o' thet old galoot. We aim to take care o' yuh now, pronto!'

Chet tensed as boots rasped on loose rock. He

125

realized the three *hombres* were sliding down the shaft. They were coming on slowly and cautiously. They were slithering forward, judging by the sounds, in a manner that suggested they were taking no chances. But they were out to get him.

Flint Randall had evidently decided to blast his opponent to boothill.

Chet figured the man was utterly ruthless. He was hard as nails. He was ignoring a wound that would have kept many a man off the saddle. Apparently Randall had got only a flesh wound in the shoulder. It was sure a pity he had not been shot into buzzard bait.

Chet gritted his teeth. He decided to take as many of the hellions as was possible with one set of guns against three.

He whipped down and turned the lantern out. He moved further back into the shaft and flattened against the wall. His eyes probed the darkness ahead, searching for the slightest indication of the first, oncoming man. His guns seemed to stare into the darkness, as if they had eyes as well as barrels which could spout flame and death.

Then in an utterly swift flash of time, guns roared.

Chet triggered slugs out in a bellowing blast as he fancied he saw a movement.

Another gun retorted – even as Chet darted to the other side of the shaft.

Chet had moved even as he had fired, for it was fool play to allow the others to pump bullets towards his gun flashes.

Slugs from the other set of guns bit into rock. The concussion in the tunnel was terrific.

Chet Duncan emptied his guns again. He had seen leaping, orange flame. The blast echoed like thunder in the confined space of the drift.

The next second a new rumble of noise added to the din.

Realizing the terrible import of what was about to happen, Chet Duncan leaped frantically right back to the blank end of the tunnel.

As he did, rock crashed down from the roof just ahead of him. Had he not leaped back, he would have been under the falling rocks.

Panting, he pressed back against the old slab of rock with the mysterious Indian symbols. Dust swirled and choked his breath. In the darkness there was just dust and confusion.

And then, as the seconds ticked on, he realized the grim position.

The roof had fallen and blocked the tunnel. Had it blocked it entirely?

Prompted by the instinct for survival, he lost no time in examining the fall of rock. He scrambled over the thick debris at the base of the fall. His outstretched hands played all around the heaped rocks. Grimly, he realized, as the seconds passed, that he could find no gap or hole in the fallen rock.

There was now no thought of Flint Randall and his hellions. The rock had cut him off from the men.

Most likely Randall and his hired gunnies had

rushed back when the rock had crashed down. Maybe the rock had thundered over the head of one of them!

Chet Duncan kept cool. He could not find a gap with his hands. He struck a match. He had found a box in Jane's shack.

The yellow light flared. Dust still hung in the air.

Chet stared at a solid wall of rock ahead. Two timbers had fallen to one side. The tunnel was completely blocked!

'Wal, ain't thet mighty fine, now,' he breathed. 'Trapped!'

He did not know or care if Flint Randall and his crew had escaped. The position was that he was entombed!

Chet turned slowly. He saw the queer signs on the slab behind him. The ancient Indian symbols seemed to mock him. They had been hidden for centuries. Now it seemed he was to be part of the old, buried remains.

He looked for the pick and lantern. He could not find them. Probably they were under the fallen rock. Grimly, he set about shifting the debris with his bare hands. He did not dare think how much rock lay ahead.

There was dead silence all around him. It was the silence of the tomb. He began to work. After some minutes there was just the rasp of boots, the panting of breath as he pulled rocks from the topmost part of the fall. With his bare hands he scooped red soil and shale away to expose the larger rocks.

For an hour he worked. He did not intend to think that this was the end. He would work on until he dropped. If his hands were torn and bleeding, he would go right on until it was impossible to work any longer.

Bitterly, he cursed Flint Randall. The man had wanted to kill him. Maybe he had succeeded!

Chet laboured until sweat dripped off him. He had tough hands, but bare flesh was not meant to be used as a shovel. He panted with the fast efforts he had been making. He stopped and struck another match. He gritted his teeth when he saw how little he had widened the tomb.

He resumed his slaving. He placed the rocks along the side of the wall. He was attempting to make a small tunnel at the top of the fall. That was the only way. He could not expect to clear all the fallen rock.

He lost all sense of time. After a while he realized some hours had passed. He knew, too, that the air was becoming deadly stale. He breathed hard all the time he worked. There was no life in the air.

He thought of Jane Bennett. At least she was fairly safe as long as she stayed with Mrs Bryant, the store keeper's wife. And Ezra Blain would be near Denver by now. A fast night ride might bring the Town Marshal to Devil's Fork tomorrow. Sheriff Brisbane would have plenty to think about when that happened. There could be no fool play with the

Town Marshal of Denver, under whose jurisdiction Tom Brisbane worked.

Chet Duncan worked and worked until he felt dazed. It was not so much the toil. The air was very bad. He gasped at each effort. His tunnel along the top of the fall had made good progress, but it was slow and laborious as the air got staler and staler.

He was working when he felt himself sway. He clawed at the rock. He was lying flat on his stomach. He opened his mouth and dragged at the air. There was no life, no relief for his panting lungs.

He drew back out of the small tunnel and lurched in the dark. With his mouth open he made harsh rasping sounds as he gasped for fresh air.

Chet Duncan did not know he slid down. Something blacked out. He slid down and huddled with dropped head.

The stale air gathered around him. He was not choking yet, but he felt terribly sleepy. Darkness eddied in his mind. He had no will-power. There was no inclination to get up.

He hardly knew how long he lay in that state. He just hovered on the verge of consciousness half the time. Blackness clawed at his mind and then sometimes ebbed. Queer noises sounded in his ears. It was a fantastic sound. Someone was knocking and tapping somewhere.

Chet Duncan groaned. He moved restlessly. Horrible weakness dragged at him. He began to drag for every breath.

The knocking sounds persisted in his ears. All at once the crazy sounds activated something in his brain. With a terrible effort he pushed himself up, slowly, swayingly. He was blind in the darkness. The fantastic knocking sounds rang all the time. He lurched to his feet and groped forward. The knocking sounds had done something to him. He grappled with one fixed idea – an idea that rose out of the mists of his mind – he must find out what was causing the sounds.

He groped towards the fall of rock and then fell against the slope. As he blundered, a current of fresh air surged to his nostrils.

Chet Duncan sensed the strangeness right down in the depths of his dazedness. He forced his mind to think, to work and shake off the deadly feeling. He sucked at the stream of air, and that helped.

His hands clawed himself to the tunnel he had made. He slid along like some burrowing animal. Then he heard the tapping sounds again and the rasp of stones as they dribbled downwards.

All the time the new air was on his face. It revived him. He brought all his will-power to bear on bringing himself to normality.

Seconds later he heard a man's voice shout from a distance. Chet burrowed into the extreme end of his tunnel and began to pull small rocks and rubble away.

He felt the air on his face stronger now. He knew there was a way out of the tomb. The air was coming in. The hole was evidently small, but he had to enlarge it and burrow through.

He worked grimly for some minutes and then heard a man's voice again. All at once hands gripped him and hauled him forward.

He did not know who was helping him. But he was getting out of the trap. Someone had dug from the other side of the fall. They had started a tunnel on the top of the slide, similar to the one he had commenced. Then, in swift moments, he was hauled through the hole, like a jack-rabbit pulled from a burrow.

A lantern suddenly surged forward as the other man swung it to get a good look at Chet.

Chet blinked in the light. A man gripped him and growled:

'Steady, feller. Yuh're one plumb lucky *hombre*!'

The man who had spoken was Fred Newton.

Chet gulped more air.

'Goldarn it, lemme git to daylight!'

'Ain't much daylight, feller,' grunted Fred Newton. 'It's sun-down right now. Still I reckon yuh feel like seeing the sky, huh?'

Chet nodded, and the two men walked forward. With every step, Chet's vigour returned. He got lungsful of good clean air.

The next moment they were at the mouth of the drift and staring at the red streaks as the sun sank on the horizon. Soon it would be dark in the desert. Maybe there would be a moon, giving the Sphinx-like mystery to the arid lands.

'How'd yuh know I was down there?' asked Chet.

'Saw yore hoss near the shack an' when I found the fall, I jest jumped to conclusions.'

'I owe yuh my life,' said Chet quietly.

'Forget it,' said the deputy. 'Thet fall wasn't too wide. Yuh were nearly out. Yuh must ha' worked like mad.'

'Guess I did. But I was slippin'. Yuh must have worked at gettin' me out yoreself. How long yuh bin hyar?'

'Half-an-hour, mebbe a little bit more.'

'What made yuh come back to this mine? Somethin' wrong? Jane Bennett is all right, ain't she?'

Fred Newton was rolling a cigarette. He handed it to Chet Duncan. Then he said flatly:

'Nope. She ain't all right. That's why I rode over here. Jane Bennett has disappeared from Devil's Fork.'

Chet shot an arm out and gripped the other's shoulder.

'What? Thet snake struck again? Goldarn it, I figgered she was safe enough with other people.'

Fred Newton struck a sulphur match and held it up for them both to light their cigarettes.

'Guess she would ha' bin iffen she hadn't bin left alone. Two riders were around behind the house at the back o' the store. No one seen them. But I saw the hoof imprints.'

'Randall!' snapped Chet. 'Why, thet *hombre* strikes more than a rattler. Let me git to my hoss.'

133

He was now fully recovered. He bounded to the saddle in a manner that showed his savage feelings. With Fred Newton, he rode away from the mine. He said nothing of his discovery of the Indian relic, but he gave an account of how Flint Randall had cornered him in the drift.

'I plugged thet jigger in the shoulder earlier. Guess he's as hard as a horse-nail. He came right back. Started shootin', and the blamed roof fell down. I shore hoped the rock had got thet man. Seems like he has more lives than a prairie dog.'

'Whar do yuh figger to ride?' rapped Fred Newton.

'Right over to Randall's mine. Thet jigger cain't git away with this. What the blazes does he figger to do with Jane?'

'I don't git it,' admitted the deputy.

Like flying phantoms in the half-light, they rode stirrup to stirrup. Crouched in the saddle, Chet pondered the situation.

'Guess thet gink figgers he kin count on me as dead,' he rapped to the deputy. 'Mebbe he aims to take Jane away an' keep her off her property fer a year – jest like his previous idea. Then he kin claim the mine. Shore likes to plan ahead, this snakeroo! Wal, his plans don't include me bein' alive. An' he don't know the Town Marshal o' Denver is ridin' this way.'

'Yuh got any idee why Randall wants thet mine?' shouted Fred Newton.

134

'I got an idee,' returned Chet. 'But I figger it's too crazy to talk about. I want to take another looksee into thet drift.'

'Heck. I should ha' figgered yuh'd had enough o' thet mine!'

'Nope. I ain't had enough. I'll tell yuh more when I kin check up. Right now I'm ridin' to git Jane offen those hellions.'

'Yuh kin count me in on thet!' snapped the other.

Shale and sand spurted under pounding hoofs. The horses sped on at a fast lope towards Flint Randall's property. The red streaks of sun-down vanished and a pale moon rode the sky.

After a fast ride that had the horses blowing, Chet and Fred Newton reached the buildings of Randall's mine.

Lights were showing in the bunkhouse and Randall's home. The two riders drew the horses close to a clump of cottonwoods and spent a few seconds watching the place. Thare seemed to be little activity at the mine. As they sat in the saddle under the trees, a burst of laughter came from the bunkhouse. Men were chuckling uproariously.

Chet listened grimly to the row.

'Sounds like a drink party goin' on.'

'How we goin' to locate thet gal?' asked Fred Newton worriedly.

'If I kin locate Flint Randall, thet'll be near enough,' rapped Chet.

He jigged his horse forward recklessly. He had one

135

idea. If he sighted Flint Randall there would be a showdown.

Chet rode down to the yard that ran around the mining property. He dismounted. Fred Newton rode up and dropped to earth as Chet walked forward silently.

Chet moved close to the bunkhouse because the building was the nearest. There was a chance Flint Randall might be there.

Plenty of noise was issuing from the place. Chet sidled along the log wall. He got to a window which was slightly open. He raised grim eyes and stared inside the log-house. Yellow light from lamps cast a glow over the rough tables and benches. About seven men were sprawling at the table, and they were playing cards. Bottles of liquor were on the table. The air was full of rowdy laughing, talk and cigarette smoke. Evidently Randall's hands were having a night on the binge!

Chet was about to pass on. He had not seen Flint Randall in the bunkhouse. Maybe the man was at his home. Randall was the boss and preferred comfort. But Chet heard a loud voice making comments.

'Yeah, reckon this about the last night fer this outfit?'

'Yep. I heerd Randall figures to fire most o' this bunch tomorrer.'

'Mebbe yuh, too, Shorty!' bawled a voice.

'Yeah, mebbe! Wal, I figgered thet bonanza was a freak all the ways. Now the lode has fallen out. Jest like thet. Once yuh got gold – next yuh got nuthin' but rock. Fallen lode, they calls it. Reckon it's fallen a hell o' a long way – mebbe a mile, by the looks o' things!'

'Aw, shut yuh yap, Shorty. Yuh ain't got much to lose. Randall ain't got nuthin' to howl for, either. He got plenty o' gold out o' thet mine!'

'Yeah? Wal, thet jigger spent it, too. Gambled! I seen thet *hombre* in Denver more'n once. Say, I c'd tell yuh . . .'

The next moment the speaker was bawled down. Seemed the others figured to spend their time gambling and not listening to talk about work.

Chet moved away, a silent, grim shadow. But he had absorbed all he had heard.

So Flint Randall's bonanza was not so good! The lode had fallen. Chet Duncan knew that this could happen. It was a freak in the strata. At some distant date in the past, there had been an upheaval which had broken the gold vein in two. By some gigantic movement, part of the vein had sank, probably under volcanic conditions. Finding the rest of the vein was practically impossible.

Chet realized this was probably the reason for Flint Randall's efforts to get possession of Jane's claim. He had wondered why the man should want more gold than he could use. He had put it down to sheer greed and lust for the power money could buy. Flint Randall still had a lust for money, and he thought there was wealth in the Bennett mine.

Maybe he was right.

Apparently Randall had known about his bonanza petering out and kept it a secret until the last minute. But his miners had found out the truth. They were a reckless bunch and probably did not care. In that there was plenty of gold – if you could find it!

Chet went up to Fred Newton and told him what lie had heard.

'Thet hellion ain't so durned wealthy. Seems he's bin gambling, too.'

'Yeah. I knew he gambled. They got roulette at Denver and high stakes. Ain't the fust *hombre* who's bin dusted out thar. Yuh didn't see Randall?'

'Nope. If I had . . .' Chet's grim words did not finish.

He intended to look in at the house. There were lights burning.

He mounted the porch with silent steps. He sidled warily to a window. Blinds were drawn. Chet listened. He wondered if he would find Flint Randall here. Maybe the man was nursing his wounded shoulder. On the other hand, maybe he was riding with his two trusties, taking Jane to some unknown destination.

The last thought made Chet coldly furious. All vestiges of a smile had gone from his lean face. The muscles around his mouth were taut. In fact, there was a killer look about him.

For Jane Bennett had come to mean something pretty fine to the young rannigan. There was something about the way she looked at him, a message in her warm brown eyes. He had realised most *hombres* had to settle and get roots some time. And it was mighty good to get roots in a ranch maybe and have a gal like Jane around.

Guns appeared in his hand. They were steady, grim. He motioned Fred Newton to stand to one side of the door.

The next second he thudded all his weight at the door. The lock catch snapped. The door burst in with a terrific crash.

Chet Duncan was in the room beyond and Colts glared. His fingers trembled on triggers.

The one man sitting in a chair jerked and then rose. He stared at the Colts in Chet's hands.

'Howdy, Sheriff Brisbane!' spat Chet.

Tom Brisbane swallowed. 'Yuh – yuh – supposed to be dead!'

'Thet what Randall told yuh!' flashed Chet.

'He said – the mine – he —'

'Yeah. I kin guess what he said. Where is the varmint?'

Tom Brisbane breathed hard.

'Yuh're pointin' thet gun at the sheriff o' Devil's Fork, feller,' he bluffed.

Fred Newton appeared around the door. His face was grave. His hands were hooked in his gun-belt.

'I'm sidin' with this man, Tom.'

'Yuh're my deputy. Yuh got a duty. This feller is wanted . . .'

'Thet ain't right,' said Fred Newton harshly.

'Those posters were printed in Devil's Fork, and I know it. Thet makes 'em false.'

'What's Randall?' snapped Chet.

Tom Brisbane suddenly put his hands in front of his face. His grizzled head sank for a moment. Then he looked up again.

'I cain't go on with this any longer,' he said haggardly. 'Randall is a dirty rat. Gawd, I ain't as bad as him! I let yuh and yore sidekick out o' jail, Duncan! I saved yuh from Randall wanting to string yuh up. Don't thet mean anythin'?'

'Yep. It means somethin',' said Chet. 'It means yuh got yore loop tangled with Randall. Wal, Tom Brisbane, thet hellion is headin' for death, an' his gold mine is pannin' out. Whar is Randall?'

'I'll tell yuh. Chet Duncan, yuh'd better git to Devil's Fork fast. Thet town is rightly named. I got into Randall's clutches in thet town. I reckon I once had a good record . . . but I took money from Randall . . . let him cover up . . . he's got papers thet could make me an outlaw . . . if the Town Marshal ever learned.'

'What's brewin' at town?' snapped Chet.

'Plenty! Randall is plannin' to marry Jane Bennett tonight! Now! Pronto!'

Chet hissed: 'Where? How?'

'In the back rooms o' the Yellow Nugget. He aims to force the preacher to marry them. He's got the gal hid away thar. No one knows thet 'sides me an' Randall's two sidekicks, Red Barton an' Al Sporn. Git goin', young feller. I hope yuh git thet fine gal away from thet devil!'

'I got advice for yuh!' snapped Chet. 'Hand over yore sheriff's badge to Fred Newton. Then hit the trail. My podner is ridin' back with the Town Marshal o' Denver tomorrow. Git goin'. Yuh kin start all over again down in Texas.'

And Chet Duncan thrust his Colts into his holsters and whipped around for the door.

He was on his horse, waiting impatiently when Fred Newton joined him again. On the man's shirt was the sheriff's star.

'Thet was the best thing to do!' snapped the new sheriff of Devil's Fork.

'Feed thet hoss steel!' rapped Chet.

They rowelled the animals and horse muscles responded. The riders sped over the moonlit land. There was no sound save the rapid tattoo of drumming hoofs. Sand and shale, thin grass and occasional mesquite bush passed swiftly by.

Then the yellow lights of the town appeared.

Chet knew Flint Randall's new plan. The man figured to marry Jane so that he could claim the mine. He would not need to wait out a year. Once the marriage was a reality, Flint Randall owned the Bennett claim – and Jane!

The last thought made Chet Duncan murderous.

They rode fast into the main stem of the town. Lights from the saloons cast patches of yellow into the dark, hard-earthed streets. Bawdy laughter rolled

141

over the streets. The lawless element took over at night. Gamblers, drinkers and rannigans simply out for trouble jostled each other in the bars and in the few noisy dancehalls.

'Whar's the Yellow Nugget?' rapped Chet to the other man.

'Nearly there. That patch o' light.'

'I'm a-bustin' in an' shootin if needed!'

'I'm supportin' yuh,' said Fred Newton. 'I'm the sheriff an' I ain't toleratin' a forced marriage.'

Grimly, Chet hoped they were not too late. The thought occurred to him: he would make Jane a widow if they were too late!

They vaulted from the horses almost before the animals slithered to a dust-raising halt. Hands over gunn butts, Chet raced for the saloon doors. He slowed as he thrust through the batwings. He did not stop. He went through the crowd of noisy customers. Little or no notice was taken of him as he shouldered through with Fred Newton immediately behind him.

Chet made for the door at the opposite end of the barroom. He guessed this led to the rooms at the back. He found himself in a passage. Fred Newton was hard at his heels. But Chet figured he was the one to bust Flint Randall's play. So he was going in first!

The passage led to a door labelled 'office'. There was another door. Chet had a hunch to look in that room.

He had a fleeting idea that the owner of the saloon

was a lawless bird like Randall. Obviously Randall was paying the owner for the use of the rooms.

Chet reached the door in three swift strides and gripped the handle. For one second he paused, heard voices. That was enough. He had heard Randall's hated voice.

Chet crashed against the door. His violence was terrific. The door went in as if a thunderbolt had struck it.

Chet Duncan was inside with the same velocity. Guns jabbed out like cannons. Two index fingers trembled on hairbreadth triggers.

Chet got an impression of a white-faced girl, a scared preacher in a black frock-coat, three men who wheeled and whipped out guns that blazed immediately.

Chet's Colts roared. And the young rannigan flung flat to the floor at the same time. Slugs spat into the air where he had stood.

Fred Newton, tense with Chet's swift play, was flat against the door-posts. Slugs nearly scorched his shirt. Red Barton dropped his guns and clapped a hand to his chest. Blood spurted through his fingers as his heart beat madly. Chet's slugs had taken him. The other *hombre* – Al Sporn – scrambled to the cover of a table, cursing his agony as a slug played hell with his innards.

Flint Randall was fast as a striking rattler.

He had whipped to Jane as soon as Chet triggered. And Chet had seen the play in a flash and turned his

143

guns off the man. He had not wanted to hit Jane.

Now Flint Randall hugged the girl before him. He had whipped her arms behind her back, and he gripped her so tightly she could not struggle away. Then Flint Randall backed towards the window.

'Don't shoot – yuh'll hit the gal shore as hell!'

Chet considered the position. He thought he might nick Flint Randall somewhere. He raised his Colts again.

'Cut it out!' snarled the man. 'I got a gun in the gal's back. Try yore tricky play an' I kill her!'

'Yuh wouldn't git far! ' breathed Chet.

'The gal would be dead,' rapped Randall. 'What's it to be?'

All the time he was backing slowly to the window.

'You can shoot to hit him!' cried the girl. 'Try it, Chet! Oh, I'm so glad you're alive!'

'Told yuh I was dead, huh! ' gritted Chet.

It was a tense scene. Flint Randall was trying a most difficult job. But he backed to the window and raised the frame easily enough.

He seemed to pause and then with a cruel push he flung Jane toward Chet. Simultaneously he slipped through the window.

NINE

Chet Duncan found Jane in his arms. He did not object to that, but the girl's sudden plunge prevented him from snapping a shot at Flint Randall. And that had been the hellion's intention.

Chet moved past Jane as swiftly as possible, and reached the window. He knew he was doing a foolhardy thing, but shoved his head out into the cool air, and looked around swiftly.

He thought he saw a shadow dashing down the side of the building. Chet snapped off two shots that roared in the night. But the shadow seemed to vanish almost with the crack of the guns. Flint Randall was having the devil's own luck.

Chet guessed the man would reach a horse. Any horse would do for the hell-bent rannigan.

Chet whipped back into the room. He saw Red Barton lying on the floor dying. Al Sporn was in little better shape. He was cursing and snarling for a doctor. The preacher was mumbling words to the men who had so recently been his enemies. Now they were just men who were dying.

'Honey, yuh all right?' Chet gripped Jane's shoulders.

Fred Newton had disappeared. Chet figured the new sheriff had run to the street in order to catch sight of Flint Randall.

'Oh, Chet I'm all right, and I'm so glad to see yuh! Oh, honey, he told me yuh were dead! He said the mine had caved in on you!'

'It did, Jane, but Fred Newton got there to help me out. Fred Newton is the new sheriff. Say, I got to dash out an' find him. Hold this gun on those jiggers. Not thet they kin do much!'

He thrust the Colt into her hands, and then he dashed out to the saloon bar. The rowdy patrons had heard the shots, but that did not matter a hoot in Devil's Fork. All that mattered was the good time.

Chet reached the street to see Fred Newton returning, gun in hand.

'Thet *hombre* got clean away!' said the new sheriff disgustedly. 'Holy smoke, yuh shore made a mess o' those other two jiggers!'

'Right an' fair!' returned Chet. He stared grimly into the darkness. 'Guess yuh're right. Randall got away. Wal, he ain't no further forward.'

'I'll git a posse an' hunt him down,' said Fred Newton. 'The feller cain't force a marriage on a gal in this town.'

'He kidnapped Jane Bennett!' snapped Chet. 'An'

he killed her father. If we kin git him, I reckon we kin pin thet on him.'

Chet Duncan went back to see Jane. He found her in the back room of the Yellow Nugget, still holding the Colt as if she intended to use it. But the two rannigans on the floor would never ride again.

Chet took the gun from the girl and led her gently out of the place. Reaction set in and she began to tremble.

'Look, honey, I'll take yuh back to yore friend, Mrs Bryant. Guess yuh'll be all right from now on.'

'I won't go out alone,' she gasped.

'Wal, Randall's side-kicks are dead or dying. Tom Brisbane is ridin' away – we gave him a chance. There's just Flint Randall left, and Fred Newton aims to corral him. Guess what I found down yore mine, Jane!'

She made the first guess.

'Gold?'

'Wal, not exactly!'

She made one or two more guesses, and then Chet figured to tell her all about finding the mysterious Indian remains. He told her everything as they walked back along the road to Mrs Bryant's home.

'Have yuh any idea what the stone slab means?' she gasped.

'Could be part o' an ancient Indian site that some-how got buried. Or mebbe it's an ancient tomb.'

'Flint Randall knows about it,' she said, with conviction. 'And it connects somehow with the slab yuh found in Randall's mine. Do yuh think he unearthed that slab from his drift?'

'Yeah. Must be thet. But Randall knows more than that. He knows what's behind the stone slab.'

Being a young girl, she could not help but be thrilled at the implication of his words.

'Oh, Chet, yuh know what's behind, don't yuh?'

'Nope. I don't!' He grinned down at her face, pretty in the moonlight. 'But I kin make a few guesses.'

'Tell me what yuh think!'

'Nope, honey. I don't figger to count chickens afore they're hatched. Now yuh got to stay safe with yore friend until I ride back. When I ride back again Randall won't be a trouble any more. And when I ride back . . . Jane . . . I . . .'

They halted outside the store. She smiled into his face.

'Yes, Chet?'

For reply, he gathered her into his arms and kissed her. For the girl it was sweet and thrilling. To Chet, it was a revelation.

Then he released her,

'By gosh, yuh kin slap my face for thet!' he breathed.

'But, Jane, when I ride back I'm goin' to ask yuh somethin'.'

'I'll be waitin' to hear it!' she whispered.

Horses, guns and rampaging hellions – Chet Duncan could handle them well enough; but this sweet girl had thrown him, and he was not yet master

148

of the situation. Soon, as befitted a man, he would be. But right now he was badly thrown.

'Doggone it!' he gasped. 'Yuh got to git indoors! Yore friends will be kinda worried. Me – I got to ride with Fred Newton.'

And in the next minute the girl found herself taken to the Bryants' door and left after a few hasty words of explanation. But Jane Bennett went indoors to safety and the knowledge that she had found a MAN even if she had not yet found gold!

Chet strode back to the saloon and grabbed at his horse. He rode back up to the main stem and beside the sheriff's office he saw Fred Newton.

'Howdy, Sheriff!' called Chet. 'I'm a-goin' over to Randall's place. Pronto. Howsabout yuh?'

'I figured to round up a posse.'

'Takes too much time. Hell, Randall is only one man. I'm a-goin' now.'

'Take it easy. I'll ride with yuh,' rapped the other. 'Yuh cain't work without the law, feller.'

'What about yore posse?'

'The blazes wi' the posse. Jest like yuh said, Randall is on his own now.'

'Git yore hoss!' roared Chet.

The other man grinned in the darkness. He strode to the hitching rail and unlooped the reins tethering his horse. With a leap, he hit saddle leather. The next moment the horse sprang into forward gallop. Chet's bay raced into a full lope and side by side they pounded down the main stem.

'Guess thet old *hombre*, Ezra Blain, is kinda late to horn in with the round-up!' shouted Chet. 'By the time thet old moseyhorn gits back, the durned play will be over!'

'Reckon yuh two would make good deputies for this town!' Fred Newton bawled back.

'Nuthin' doin', pal! I got some new ideas when this play is over.'

'How about Ezra Blain?'

'Thet old jigger!' roared Chet. 'Why, I guess it's time he settled down!'

Fred Newton chuckled distinctly above the drum of horses' hoofs.

Once again they rode fast over the arid land between Devil's Fork and Flint Randall's one-time bonanza. They could not be sure the man had returned to his place, but it was a good guess. If Flint Randall decided the game was played out, he would want to ride to his home in order to collect some money.

If Flint Randall had any sense – and the hellion was not exactly a fool – he would realize that Devil's Fork was too hot for him. He had seen that Fred Newton was siding with Chet Duncan. A little horse-sense would soon force on the man the realization that he had over-played his hand. The odds were that Flint Randall would take to the trail.

The two horsemen rode hard for the mine. The horses responded gallantly, although Chet's bay was tired. The day had been hard on the animal.

The first thing they saw was a light burning in the house. That might mean something or nothing.

Chet was first to leap from his horse. He threw the reins over a corral fence. Another second and he was a grim, vengeful figure striding through the moonlight. Fred Newton was soon after him. With Chet's swift actions, it seemed the new sheriff was always behind Chet. That was no fault of his own. Chet had lightning reaction and decision.

The next moment Chet saw the two horses saddled and hitched to the tie-rail outside the house. Chet paused, darted to one side and came walking swiftly up to the side of the house. He halted in the shadow of the building. Fred Newton came moving up, silently as a stalking animal.

Guns were in hands. They stared at the house door. The waiting horses were significant. Sooner or later someone would come out to ride away.

One horse was already loaded with two small bags slung on each side of the saddle. Chet could make a good guess as to the contents. There would be gold dust and grub, or maybe spare clothes. Somebody was all set for a getaway.

Over to the right, some hundred yards away, the noise still issued from the bunkhouse. The miners were unaware of the night's events. If Randall was all set to make a ride, Chet wondered what the miners would think. Maybe Randall owed them wages!

The next moment the door opened. Flint Randall lurched out. One arm was hanging limp, as if it hurt to move it. Chet grinned thinly. That was the shoulder he had plugged. Well, the hour had arrived when a shoulder wound would be the least of Flint Randall's troubles.

Chet called softly: 'Randall! Hoist'em!'

For answer, the man crashed backwards in a truly gigantic leap.

Guns crashed in the night. Chet's Colts had bellowed. Randall's had scooped and fired all in one frantic movement.

Chet marvelled grimly. He ought to have hit the man. Randall had cleared the slugs by less than a hair.

The door of the house was now slammed shut. A bar was heard to fall into place.

Flint Randall had barricaded himself in!

Chet raised his guns and threw some shots at the window. A rataplan of fire snapped back at him. Then the light in the house went out. Randall had extinguished the lamp in case he was revealed against it.

As the echoes died away, Chet snapped grimly to Fred Newton:

'Thet jigger gits by better than the devil!'

Fred Newton tapped Chet's arm.

'I'm a-goin' around to the back.'

He hurried away. Chet watched the front grimly. He did not like the set-up. Flint Randall might yet escape but with Fred Newton at the rear of the house, it would not be so easy.

At the sound of the shots, men tumbled from the bunkhouse. Chet turned his back to the wall of Randall's home and faced them with two guns.

One man roared: 'What's goin' on hyar?'

They saw Chet Duncan and stopped.

Chet rapped back: 'Git to yore cards, *hombres*. This is a private party. The law is after Flint Randall. He's wanted for murder and other charges. Any man who sides with Randall is actin' against the law.'

'Who the hell are yuh? Yuh ain't the law.'

'I'm workin' with Fred Newton, an' he's the sheriff of Devil's Fork now!' snapped Chet.

'Whar the blazes is Fred Newton?'

'On the other side o' this durned house!' roared Chet. 'Cain't yuh see two hosses over there? Cain't yuh see Randall's hosses saddled and loaded for his getaway? Thet jigger aims to ride tonight. He's leavin'.'

A combined growl went up from the men. They were rough and tough, and, unlike Red Barton, Al Sporn and Myers Stultz, were not Randall's confidants. They were mostly hired hands.

'Thet galoot owes us wages!' bawled one man.

'Yuh bet. What about our dinero?'

'Git around this house an' see thet Randall doesn't run for it!' rapped Chet. 'You'll git yore wages when thet jigger's affairs are cleared up.'

The men acted on that. Quickly they had surrounded the house. A few began to bawl for Flint Randall. Others shouted threats. Randall could not fail to hear them. His men had turned against him. Evidently he had figured to leave them in the lurch.

Chet shouted during a lull.

'Come on out, Randall! The play is finished!'

A snarl answered him. Chet smiled thinly. So Randall was still in the house. He would never get away now.

'The marshal from Denver will ride into town tomorrow!' roared Chet. 'Yuh'll git a trial. Yuh'll git a fair hearin'.'

For answer, a volley of rifle fire snapped from the house. Flint Randall had got himself a rifle.

All at once a drunken miner started a new turn of events. It was something Chet had not bargained for.

A red flame suddenly shot to the roof. A miner had flung a burning stick to the roof of the house. It was the sort of stupid thing a violent man might do in a temper. It seemed he had found some tar, dipped the stick into it and lighted it.

Chet started forward angrily. There was no need for crazy destruction. Hardly had he moved when another burning brand shot on to the wood roof.

Chet looked around grimly for a ladder. He had some idea of knocking the burning sticks from the roof. But he could not find one. And there was no water handy.

Inside the next swift minute, the roof was alight. Chet muttered angrily. Staring up, he knew there was no chance of putting the blaze out now. Few of the other miners seemed inclined to assist.

Chet stationed himself in the yard opposite the front door to Randall's house. The man was in a trap. At any moment he would be forced to run out. There was no alternative, unless he decided to burn alive.

The crackle of flames rose in the night air. The bone-dry timber was catching alight with terrible speed. A red glare surrounded the roof of the house.

Chet shouted: 'Randall! Come on out! The house is alight!'

He figured the man would know that well enough. He shouted again: 'Yuh'll git a trial. But I warn yuh, I aim to stick Frank Bennett's death on yore hide!'

Grim, hard words, but he was dealing with a brutal man.

The door did not open. Randall did not dash out. Instead another burst of rifle fire caused Chet to duck. It seemed Flint Randall was crazy with rage. All his plans had shattered, and Chet Duncan was the *hombre* responsible.

But the rifle fire was flung wildly and came nowhere near Chet Duncan.

The fire crackled and leaped down the sides of the house. Suddenly some of the roof fell in. The timber was being consumed with terrible speed. Randall would have to emerge or die.

Ten tense minutes later, Flint Randall opened the door of his burning house and lurched out.

Chet went into a crouch. Hands hovered over gun butts.

'Throw down yore gun, Randall!' he rasped across

155

the yard. The grim words carried across the crackle of burning wood.

'Yuh kin go to hell!' snarled Flint Randall, and his already outstretched Colt exploded.

Chet Duncan's incredible draw beat the other man. Chet had holstered his guns when he had attempted to find a ladder.

Randall had fired with the first word of his retort to Chet. And Chet had known the man would fire.

The young rannigan had scooped and triggered all in one amazing movement. Although a split second behind, he beat the other's gun.

Chet's slug took Flint Randall in the chest. Randall's shot veered slightly with the impact of the slug against the gun-holder. The slug sang over Chet's shoulder and sped harmlessly into the night.

Flint Randall had no more chances. With a slug in his chest, he dropped his gun. He stood swaying, an expression of incredulity on his harsh features. Then slowly, like a lifeless dummy, he toppled forward and thudded against the dusty yard.

Chet Duncan stared with sombre face. There was nothing about this that he liked. There was no fun in killing a man, even if the man was a murderous devil.

Slowly, he holstered his Colts. He stared at the gun butts. For an odd moment he wondered if the time had arrived for him to hang the guns up. Surely there were other ways of living?

But, looking at the man, now already dead, he decided that justice had been served. Randall had attempted to gun his way out and failed.

The miners crowded around as soon as the word got around. Most of them were hardened rascals, and the sight of Flint Randall was nothing to them. It was still fixed in their minds that the man owed them back wages.

Fred Newton came around and stared down at the dead man.

'Wal, thet shore fixes thet! Ain't much he kin do now!'

'He killed Frank Bennett,' said Chet slowly. 'I'm shore about thet. This is a just end.'

Chet turned and grabbed at his horse's reins. Slowly, he rode back over the arid lands. Fred Newton did not accompany him this time. The new sheriff stood back to control the miners and wait until the blaze had died down.

Only once did Chet turn in the saddle. He saw the red glow on the distant sky. Then, thinking of Jane, he turned again. A smile crept back to his lips. He rode on towards Devil's Fork.

It was next day when Ezra Blain, as expected, rode into Devil's Fork accompanied by the Town Marshal of Denver. They had been riding most of the night. Chet Duncan and Jane were there to greet the old-timer as he rode down the trail into the town.

As they met on the trail, horses halted. Chet was near enough to lean forward and slap Ezra's back.

'Why, yuh doggone old coot, yuh look mighty healthy! What the heck yuh bin doin' in Denver? Jest

157

havin' a good time, I reckon, while I rode the hoofs offen this cayuse!'

'I bin workin'!' roared Ezra. 'Heck, I might ha' had jest one little drink in Denver, but thet was all. Yuh kin ask the Town Marshal!'

They rode back into Devil's Fork, and there Fred Newton, wearing the sheriff's badge, greeted the party. A lot of explanations were handed out, and everyone was wised up. More important, the names of Chet Duncan and Ezra Blain were cleared completely. Outside the sheriff's office, the Town Marshal of Denver tacked a notice which cleared the two men of any stigma.

'There's jest one thing,' said the Town Marshal. 'Why the blazes did Randall want to control the Bennett claim?'

Chet smiled around the group.

'He figured there was gold there, an' mebbe he was right.'

'Gold! Is thet claim goin' to be a bonanza?' exclaimed Fred Newton.

'I cain't rightly say,' said Chet. 'Yuh'll have to give us podners a few more days. We've got work to do.'

And he grinned at Jane Bennett and Ezra Blain.

Some time later they rode back to Jane's shack. They went into the mouth of the drift and stared at the fall of rock.

'We got to clear thet,' announced Chet. 'We got to open this mine right back.'

He told Ezra everything, and that included the

facts concerning his discovery of the Indian finds.

'Shore seems a lot o' work!' groaned Ezra.

'Yuh ain't worried about a little work. Goldarn it, we've got to find what lies beyond the Indian remains.'

'Jest when I figgered to git meself a drop o' likker in town!' groused Ezra, and then he scratched his whisker stubble and grinned at them. He even winked at Jane. For two days the men worked at clearing the shaft. Then they dug all around the big slab of ancient rock adorned with the ancient symbols. They got the slab out by means of levers.

There was a definite, stone-slabbed passage beyond. It needed no excavation. Chet and Ezra were the first to move into the passage. It was a strange feeling to know that hundreds of years had passed since man had walked into the passage.

They found a vault at the end. It presented an incredible sight. There was gold – but not raw gold and quartz. The vault was stacked with tarnished ornaments of an ancient Indian origin, and they were solid gold. They stood in grotesque nooks and crannies of the old vault, just as they had been placed hundreds of years ago, before white men had set foot on the continent. The value was tremendous!

'Gold! An' Randall knew it was hyar!' exclaimed Chet. 'I got the hunch, too, but it was kinda crazy.'

'Don't look crazy to me – podner!' guffawed Ezra. It was a lot later, when claim to the gold had been filed with the authorities, that Chet discovered that the slab in Randall's drift had really been taken from the Bennett mine. Randall had stolen it and had the symbols deciphered by an old Indian. The symbols were really a key to the vault. Randall had known the truth then. So had Frank Bennett, but had left the telling too late. He had died before he had had time to tell Jane.

Chet stood by the girl one night, when a great many things had been cleared up. Red streaked the sky, making a lovely sundown.

But Chet was very tongue-tied. It was only when Jane stood so close to him that he could do no other than put his arms around her, that another detail was cleared up.

Chet Duncan was about to get roots! And he figured it was a mighty fine prospect!

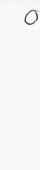